K-9 5.98

D1298552

GOODBYE TO ELSA

Goodbye to Elsa

SAROS COWASJEE

new press

TORONTO 1974

ISBN 0–88770–206–6

new press
Order Department
553 Richmond Street West
Toronto M5V 1Y6, Ontario

Manufactured in England

'Oho!' they cried, 'The world is wide,
But fettered limbs go lame!
And once, or twice, to throw the dice
Is a gentlemanly game . . .'

OSCAR WILDE
The Ballad of Reading Gaol

1

There were fireworks that night. In my left eye. I tumbled out of bed and, afraid of the light, staggered my way to the armchair where I threw my gown each night. I got my right arm into the sleeve, and I tied the cord round my waist. You don't need eyes for that. My wife followed me about repeating 'What is it now?' and I heard the child howl as I slammed the door of the car. Covering my eye with the palm of my left hand, I drove through lights red and green to the Emergency Ward.

Under a pale light a nurse was poring over a file. 'Come in the morning,' she told me. I insisted. An intern appeared and diagnosed what I had feared.

I had saved $2,000 and I wanted the best surgeon. I wanted to go to Toronto, Frankfurt, Zurich, but the doctors told me that they must operate on me immediately, that the best surgeon was here. I could keep my money, for my medical insurance was in order. Would I pay $25 as a deterrent fee?

A week later I walked out of the hospital, with my toothbrush and pyjamas. The surgeon's average had gone down by one per cent (it was eighty-five, he told me, when he laid me on the table) and I had lost an eye. The other eye was good, he said, if I took care. With my good eye I could see enough to get back home, enough to leave my wife and child, more than enough to hide from all the eyes of the world.

I had not planned on being here. It all happened the day I walked back home. Killing had not occurred to me then. But when my wife answered the door and kissed me on the blind eye, the full horror of my fate dawned on me. And the sight of my one-year-old son confirmed my fears. He lay there on the cot, a steady trickle of saliva running down his chin; ugly, twisted, helpless, with his brown, beady eyes. Mercy? No thank you. It was as much a part of God's design as mine. I have prayed and wept, wept and fasted. But that was a long time ago.

'Elsa, sit down,' I said to my wife. 'No, not here. I want you to sit in that chair and listen to every word I say.'

She sat before me with her arms folded, seeming to read my thoughts. That's her way. One of the things that led me to marry her was the notion that she could read my thoughts. No good going into that now: I have turned it over in my mind many times as I lay sleepless beside her. Long, sleepless nights, when you hold your breath and hear the other breathing.

I will have to shut only one eye now. Easier still—push the barrel down your throat and don't count.

2

I have been here a week now. It is August and hot. I opened the bedroom window for the first time today to let in a bit of fresh air. But I keep the sun out. I occasionally peep from behind the curtains. The valley lies before me like a whore, divided by the rich undergrowth which hides her menstrual flow. They call it the River Quimperle. I want to go and piss in it before it is frozen. And I want to go down to the store and buy a dozen tins of sardines. But they close the store at six and the sun does not go down until nine. In winter it will be different. It will be dark by five and all will be well. And I shall dare it in the day too, when the wind shall rise and blow the snow into their ugly faces and send them scurrying home with cold arses. I shall go to the post office, too, and write my farewell to Elsa:

Farewell, farewell! but this I tell
To thee, thou Wedding-Guest!

I am a perfectionist; I never make mistakes. I work out my plans to the last detail, and the total effect is that of a miniature Rajput painting. Every hair is etched, the pubic hair not excluded. Elsa shaves, and I don't care. Besides, I won't paint her. I am not an artist, I am a historian. I shall get my full salary for the next three months, and then sixty per cent till I kill myself. After that Elsa can collect $30,000 from my insurance. I don't grudge her anything as long as she keeps her mouth shut.

When I got Elsa to sit down and listen to me, I made her take down my proposal point-wise, hair by hair, and got her to sign it—Elsa William Elliott. The document, a copy of

3

which I carry in my wallet, reads: 'I hereby swear to observe the following rules of conduct: (a) never to attempt to get in touch with you or to find out where you are, (b) to inform the College that you have gone to London for eye treatment, (c) to keep pretending that I hear from you and that you are improving, (d) to remain within a radius of ten miles of the house'.

In return for these services I promised Elsa that I should be back home in six months. I then contacted a friend, who now lives in Kamloops, and rented his farm-house on a hillside overlooking Corwind. I got my few clothes and all my letters and papers into a suitcase and sent for a taxi. At this point Elsa broke down and crumpled into a heap. She begged me not to go, or at least to tell her where I was going. For a moment I felt like relenting and staying, but when Elsa said, 'What is an eye? People who lose both eyes live on,' I knew I had to go. Go, while the going was good. I silenced Elsa with a stare from my good eye, though I don't discount the help I might have got from my blind one.

I asked the cab-driver to stop at the Army and Navy store where I bought a .22 rifle and five hundred cartridges. I then asked him to drive me North.

'Where?' he asked.

'North,' I said.

He refused to move until I gave him my destination. I refused to budge until he drove me to my destination. 'Fuck you,' he said, and threw me out of the cab. This was a blessing in disguise, for it struck me that five hundred cartridges were not enough for a lifetime. I went back to the store and bought another five hundred. Also, if I had kept the same cab, Elsa could have got hold of the driver and found my whereabouts. You don't know Elsa; she is like a police dog: give her a whiff and she will smell you right up to your ass-hole and then—wow.

I got into another cab and asked the driver to take me north. The same old bloody question again.

'To Corwind,' I told the inquisitive bastard.

He didn't want to go to Corwind. I tipped him five dollars and he began changing his mind. He told me he didn't like

4

my sitting in the back seat with a gun in my hand. I obliged him by letting him lock my gun in the car trunk, and by coming and sitting beside him.

'Would you be returning from Corwind, sir?' he asked as we turned on to Highway 17.

'No.'

'If you are coming back in a short while, sir, I could wait for you.'

'No.'

'You won't find a cab in Corwind to bring you back.'

I held on to my patience; you learn to do that in Canada. These Canadians are so irritatingly obtuse. I felt defenceless without my gun. I wanted to get out and hunt for another taxi, but it was getting late. And I had already given the bastard five dollars. Above all, the fellow was no longer asking: 'Where?'

I stuck it out. At an intersection a couple of miles from Corwind I alighted, paid off the cab, and settled down by the roadside with my gun and suitcase. I didn't want to go to the house before dark; too many prying eyes in the prairies. Four cars stopped and asked me if they could drop me somewhere. That's the way with Canadians. They are always ready to give you a ride when you don't want one. Last winter, when I forgot to plug in my car, I almost froze to death walking to College in one of those moaning, howling blizzards. Only my hatred of my colleagues kept me warm and alive. And not a bloody car stopped though I waved both arms till I burst open my coat at the armpits. When I told Elsa about Canadian inhumanity, she said she had always maintained that the Army and Navy stuff was no good, that in future I should shop at the Bay.

I entered Mountain View—that's what the house is called —at ten past ten. The house is well-furnished and has all the space I need: four bedrooms, one living-room, one dining-room, one kitchen, one garage and one basement. The back-yard is big and fenced. It needs a coat of paint, and there is enough paint in the basement. Also, do-it-yourself tools. I spent the first three days in the basement, but found it difficult to breathe there. I now live, sleep, eat and write in the living-room. I prefer the living-room for the curtains are sun-proof. I keep the lights on day and night. I don't sleep much.

Perfectionist that I am, I made two very serious mistakes. I forgot to consider my dead body; I should have ordered a coffin and made my funeral arrangements before I came here. I cannot bear to see myself lying dead on the sofa, rotting, smelling, with a 'convocation of politic worms' at me. Worse, I forgot to bring food to last me while I am here. I have finished the odd tins of beans, tomato sauce and noodle soup which I found in the kitchen cupboard. There is a jar of apple jam left in the fridge. I don't know what to do. The nearest grocery store is two miles away, and there are people about.

3

It is night. I have not had anything to eat for four days. The grocer was to deliver the food this afternoon, but he didn't come. I don't feel hungry, but there is a slight pain and a rumbling noise in my belly. I hope he will come tomorrow. I don't want to go down to the store again.

I walked to Corwind this morning. Had to. There was nothing in the house. To avoid being recognised, I applied some red paint below my lips and wrapped a silk scarf around my face. A dust-storm was brewing, and I walked with my head bent. I did not see anything save a few cars that sped past. I recall passing a gas station and the R.C.M.P. barracks. The trip took me over forty minutes.

There was nobody in the store except an old woman. She had small beady eyes, peering through steel-rimmed glasses. She had a sharp nose and a receding chin, and her hair was tied in a bun on the top of her head. May have been good-looking once. She had a kindly, inquisitive face.

To avoid unnecessary conversation, I began placing my order as soon as I entered. Four pounds of ground beef, two pounds of pork chops, leg of lamb, five pounds of potatoes, three pounds of rice, a pound of peas, one pound of beans, six loaves of bread, salt, pepper, ginger, turmeric, garlic, coffee and sugar.

'Would that be all?' she asked.

'Yes. Could I have a dozen tins of sardines?'

'We've sold out of sardines, but my husband has gone to get some from Erigon.'

'When will he be back?'

'In about an hour or so. You come back, or we'll have it sent to your place.'

'Can you have all the stuff delivered by the afternoon?'

'Oh, yes. Where do you live?'

I felt trapped. It hadn't occurred to me that if he came to deliver the groceries he would find out where I lived. But I took courage. Let him find out—I had a gun.

'I live in Mountain View.'

'Oh, you do, do you? Then you know the Mises. They are in Kamloops, I hear. Bought all their groceries here. They were a nice couple, they were.'

'Yes, they are a nice couple,' I repeated after her, looking at the shelves to see if I had missed anything I needed. But I could not see too well. Was my other eye failing? Later, I found that it was always a little too dark in the store.

'Raise your hand,' I demanded. 'Now open out your fingers. Not all.'

She obeyed without questioning. I covered my left eye with my palm, and called: 'That's four.'

'Sure,' she answered, relaxing. 'What's wrong with your eyes?'

'Wait,' I said. I covered my right eye and asked her to repeat the act. I couldn't see a thing.

'How many do you see now?' she asked, good-humouredly.

'Eight.'

'That's twice what I showed.'

'True. Very true. Eight and four are twelve. Twelve in all. Please, how much do I owe you?'

She began to add up on an old machine. My gaze fell on a white can on the counter on which was written in red letters: CANCER CAN BE BEATEN.

'May I have that can?' I asked.

'It's for donations. What would you want it for?'

'Please give it to me,' I said.

'I will give you another can.'

'No. Sell that to me. I will give you a dollar for it.'

She emptied the can of the few pennies that were in it and gave it to me—free. I told her that I would take it with me if she would put it in a bag. I then paid her seventeen dollars and twenty-nine cents. As I was leaving the store she asked me the question I most dreaded.

'What do you do?'

I felt like telling her to mind her own business, which was certainly not to find out what her customers did. But she was a kindly person, and she had given me the can free and put it in a bag for me.

'I am a writer,' I said.

'Oh,' she beamed. 'A writer! I always told my husband that Corwind would have a writer one day. It's so peaceful and quiet here. What do you write?'

'I am writing a story.'

'Is it a love story?'

'There is love in it,' I answered. 'And there is murder.'

'Now, don't talk about murder in Corwind. We've been here for thirty years and there hasn't been a killing. Yes, small thefts, yes, at times. They broke into our store two summers ago and got away with the cash box. But no murder. It's one of the few places left where they don't go about killing.'

'True,' I said, and stalked out. On the way back I wondered why she hadn't asked me why I kept my face covered. I removed the scarf but could not rub off the paint. So I wound it again, and with head bent, hastened home. I parted the curtains of the living-room for five minutes to let the sun in.

4

I had placed the CANCER-CAN-BE-BEATEN can against the fence in a far corner of the back-yard and was taking shots at it from my bedroom window. I had not handled a gun for three years: the last time I did so was when I wounded a hare. It cried out like a human baby, and after that I gave up hunting. Though out of practice I was doing well, averaging a hit in every three shots. I was getting used to the gun, when someone called out, 'Hi.'

The gun dropped from my hand and fell on the ground under the window. Elsa had got me at last.

'Who's there?' I called out.

A head popped over the fence. 'It's me. I have brought you your groceries.'

'Come to the front door.'

A girl in a yellow skirt and a white blouse stood with a large parcel in her arms. She was full-bodied, moon-faced, light brown hair done up with a green ribbon, eyes big and beautiful.

I took the parcel from her. 'Come in,' I said.

She looked at her boots which were caked with mud. She was fumbling for words when I asked her to remove her boots and step in. She obeyed as if it were the most natural thing to do. I opened the parcel on the table beside my typewriter and put the meat and the vegetables in the fridge.

'Where are the sardines?'

'I don't know. Mother wrapped up the parcel and asked me to bring it here.'

'I paid for a dozen tins of sardines. Will you remind your mother?'

'Yes.' And she moved towards the door.

'Sit down. I'll make you some coffee.'

She agreed hesitantly, sitting nervously on the edge of a chair. I put the kettle on the stove.

'What is your name?'

'Marie, Marie Germain.'

There was an awkward silence. I waited for her to ask me my name. She didn't.

'You haven't asked me my name,' I said at last.

'What's your name?'

'I won't tell you now.'

'Why?'

'Because you didn't ask me first.'

'Tell me.'

'My name is legion, for we are many.'

She stood up. 'I think I'd better be going.'

'Sit down,' I said firmly. 'Do you take cream and sugar?' She did not answer.

'There is no cream. But you can have sugar.' And I handed her the cup.

I stood leaning against the wall, looking at her. She was indeed a very beautiful girl; tense, nervous, the cup in her hand shook and her lips quivered even as she bit them. I suddenly felt cruel towards her, the sort of cruelty I have often felt towards the weak and the innocent—towards my son.

'What do you feel, Marie, sitting alone with a stranger in his house? A stranger whose name you do not know!'

'You asked me in,' she said. And after a while, 'Mother said you were a writer.'

'I am Alpha and Omega, the beginning and the end, the first and the last. Do you want to hear a story?'

'I should go . . .'

'It was five years ago. Five years ago there was a girl called Nellie. We were both students in Delhi: she at Miranda House and I at St Stephen's. I loved her very much; I wanted to marry her. We spent our evenings together. She looked like you, and she was as tall as you are and she was as beautiful as you are. Her eyes, too, were like yours; her feet were like yours—large and claw-like. That's how she used to describe them, "claw-like".'

Marie crossed her feet and tried to hide them under her chair.

'Don't, Marie. They were like yours, and she too used to hide them the way you do. Then she didn't have to hide them any more. Yes, I forgot. She used to come to my room and go straight to the bath to wash her feet. Then she would come and stand before me bare-footed. I would remove her clothes one by one, till she stood naked before me. Then I would lift her up and lay her on my bed—on her back . . .'

'Why are you telling me this?' said Marie, standing up.

'Sit down and don't move. Don't move an inch.'

Marie sat down, looking awfully pale. Did she fear I would harm her? Stretch her on the bed?

'The ritual would begin. I would take her feet in my hands and press them together and kiss them. I would kiss her toes several times and then I would move up, inch by inch, kissing the length of her legs till I came to her sex. We never had sex, it didn't seem important. I would continue the journey, pausing awhile on her breasts, neck, chin and lips. I would rest on her lips, rub my nose against her nose, and lick her eyes. Her eyelashes would glisten with my saliva. It took fifteen minutes each time by the watch. I used to keep my watch beside her on the bed and time it. Fifteen minutes to the dot. Didn't have to buy an alarm clock. In fifteen minutes I would traverse the entire length of her body, leaving nothing unkissed.'

Marie stared at me, frightened. She asked me why I was weeping. I wiped my eyes with my sleeves and laughed. I didn't tell her one couldn't weep with one eye.

'During the summer she went home to Bombay. A friend of hers—a girl at school—told me Nellie had had an accident. She was getting on to the train when she slipped, and the wheels went over her legs.

'I wrote several letters to Nellie to find out what had happened and how she was. But there was not a word from her. Finally, I took the train to Bombay and rushed to her flat. Her family was away and a servant let me in. Nellie was sitting in a chair, just as you are sitting there. A blue blanket lay on her lap. Do you want to hear more?'

Marie did not reply. She was breathing heavily.

'Nellie looked at me with her large brown eyes dimmed with tears. She did not utter a word. I came forward to kiss her, but she pushed me away with her arms. Then she lifted the blanket. Do you know what I saw? I saw two stumps, red stumps, where the knees were. Red and raw, protruding out towards me . . .

'I would now have to kiss her from the knees up. She would not have to wash her feet again, and in all it would take only ten minutes now . . .'

'Why? Why must you talk like that?' cried Marie.

I felt sorry for her. 'Why Marie? Two stumps and a whole life! Do you know how long a life is?'

'No.'

'Ten minutes. I have not been able to time it for Nellie pushed me away.'

'Why did she do that?'

'Because the ritual must take fifteen minutes. Do you understand?'

'No,' screamed Marie, her face flushing a vivid pink. 'You are mad, completely mad. Mother told me so: you made her raise her hand and saw eight fingers on it.'

'I ran into the streets. There were no people—nothing but grinning faces; rows and rows of horrible grinning faces. I ran faster. I turned here and there, but wherever I went there were more faces—just senseless, endless, jeering faces. I could go no further. The Georgian and Victorian mansions with their huge colonnades and balustrades cast their shadows about me, and on the pavement there were at last people who were not laughing at me. They were all huddled together, and they all looked alike. There were the blind, the armless and the legless; there were lepers who had raked up their sores to bleed for human sympathy. They were all begging, but there was one who did not beg. He lay as if asleep, his hands clutching on to his bowl. I threw a coin at him. It rolled and came to rest against his hollow cheek. But he made no effort to pick it up.

'Another beggar, with a bemused expression on his face,

shook his head. Seeing that I made no move to retrieve the coin, he slid on his haunches and picked it up. He blessed me.

' "It's for that man. Not for you," I said.

' "Ah, for him," he said, shaking his head again. "You should have given him yesterday, then, my Master."

' "Why?"

' "He is dead. He has found release."

' "Dead?"

' "Died in the early hours of the morning—of hunger. We both sat here, as we had done every day since the last three monsoons. He was getting old and weak, much too weak to stretch out his arms and ask for food. Many people passed by. Kind people, good people, who would give if you ask them. I told him he would die if he didn't beg. But it was useless talking to him. He sat there dumb: there—where he lies now. In the evening he closed his eyes. I heard him cough before sunrise. That was the last I heard him." '

'I approached the body. It was naked but for a piece of jute round the middle, which hid nothing. There was no flesh on him, just skin, which preserved and held his skeleton together. Swarms of flies were feasting on the corpse, converging on the sockets of the eye, the half-opened lips, and the yellow between the thighs. The earth around his waist was damp. He had urinated. Flies congregated there as well.

'I fled. At last I came to the beach where children were making castles in the sand. I sat down and watched the children. I joined them in their play. I too had built castles when I was a little boy.'

I could not continue. Marie got up and looked at me for half a minute or so. Then without a word she put on her boots and left.

I watched her graceful figure go down the path which met the road that led to Corwind, and the world outside. She walked slowly, pensively, reluctantly—as if she did not want to go. But she did not once look back.

5

A month after Nellie threw away her legs, I left India. There was not much to leave. Father, a British pilot, had been shot down over Burma during the last days of the war. I was then four years old. I don't recall Father now: to my mind he is always associated with things going up in flames. I often wonder why he didn't bail out, as did his co-pilot. What, had he lived? What would my life have been? I love my father, but I am glad he is dead. I couldn't live any other life but the one I am living.

Mother? She is alive and well. Still a nurse at Willingdon Hospital, where she met Father. Mother is Anglo-Indian, which makes me three-quarters English. Mother has kept her job, though we were well provided for. It helped her to tide herself over Father's death, and later to find other men to enliven her evenings. Mother never demeaned herself: her lovers were always English or Eurasians. It was hard at times, when there were more colonels in Delhi than Anglo-Indian girls. And Mother was beautiful.

Brothers, sisters, friends?—None. Love, yes. Nellie, my love, my life. What did they do with your legs? Did they bury them? Or did they give them to the medicos to cut them up? One leg in deep freeze: the big toe, the long toe, the middle toe—1 2 3 4 5. I hope the stumps will go brown, the colour of your skin. I didn't like the raw, red look. The doctor should have trimmed them even, one seemed a little longer to me. Comfy and cosy you will sit in a chauffeur-driven car. At Marine Drive you will sit and watch the waters break upon the rocks. Beggars—armless and legless—will come to you, and you will drop coins into their bowls. They will bless you, my lovely Nellie. And I shall love you for ever and for ever.

It was a one-class boat we took to London: the *Canton*. It was packed with Australians, but at Bombay it seemed as though the Indians had taken over the ship. There were Indians here and Indians there, there were Indians everywhere. Three hundred of them—all for higher studies abroad. The more enterprising among them will come to own restaurants in London and Glasgow and provide jobs for their less fortunate brethren.

East and West met on the sea, as I had never seen them meet on land. Sexually inhibited East opened up its *dhoti* (loin-cloth) at the first contact with the West. It met the crew on an equal footing: standing drinks to every white porter and waiter. Bare legs and white thighs. The sun-deck was tanned with Indians ogling every female under fifty. But the West refused to cohabit; the boat began to pitch and roll. The Raos, the Sharmas, the Vermas had had enough. Before we called at Aden, they had dispersed. They had retired to their cabins to masturbate.

It was raining the day I arrived in Dublin. It was raining the day I left Dublin. In the three months I was there, there were only three days when it did not rain. I had a taste of what was going to be so characteristic of Dublin life even before I touched the shores of Ireland. On a cold morning, my cabin-mate hustled me on to the deck of the Liverpool–Dublin boat, saying, 'You'll see th' Wicklow Mountains now! Nothin' in th' worl' like it, I say.' And pointing his finger towards the horizon, he exclaimed, 'Ther', jus' behin' th' mist . . . th' clouds, you see . . . behin' th' clouds are th' Wicklow Mountains. . . . Mos' beautiful!'

Later, he told me that though he had been on the deck a dozen mornings looking out for the mountains, he had not seen them himself.

I liked mountains—when I was a boy. I liked rivers and trees, but I don't care for them any more. Sunsets still gladden me, but how many sunsets will I see? The loaded gun stands in the corner, but don't get me wrong. I am not ready to die. It is easy to die, and I don't do anything that is easy. Besides, as I said earlier, I need a coffin. I also need—I forgot to mention—incense.

It was hard to find a room for the sum I could afford as rent. But I found a cellar newly papered. The landlady told me that it was the warmest room in Dublin and anywhere else I would surely die of the cold. Nor have I forgotten her immediate anxiety, 'How long ar'e goin' to sthay here?' I told her it would all depend on the books available at Trinity College and the National Library. 'Ah, then it's goin' to be a long, long while,' she said with satisfaction. 'Them places are full of books an' when you've rhed them all, come to me, for I've some.' She was a Catholic—never missed Mass on Sunday—but she kept reminding me that she was an atheist so I might not rely on her Christian charity and get away with a week's rent.

Next door was Sullivan's Café and General Store. Sullivan is a swine I shall never forget. It was on a Sunday morning I stumbled into his shop.

'What's the price of butter?'

'Three-and-nine for you, sir.'

'Eggs?'

'Four-and-six for you, sir.'

For everything I asked there was the clear, emphatic 'for you, sir'. And I had noticed that he said that to none of his other customers. Kindness—Irish kindness, I thought. Has guessed from my clothes that I am not rich, and from my appearance that I am a foreigner, and wishes to be good to me. Anxious to repay a good turn, I was in the shop every day, buying most of the things I needed—and some of the things I didn't. All because they were cheaper here with 'for you, sir' thrown in free. It was about the time I was leaving Dublin that I discovered to my chagrin that with every 'for you, sir' he was charging me more than he charged the others.

I was lonely, and unhappy. I thought of Nellie most of the time, and of my mother—occasionally. Mother was lonely like me, finding temporary escape in middle-aged white paunches. Thinking of Nellie and my mother, it occurred to me that there was no escape for them. And there was no escape for me either, for I was a part of them. I began suffering from insomnia. I took to drinking, and I drank hard. Bottle after bottle of stout. But the insomnia persisted all night, and the day seemed empty.

I went to the free clinic on Rathmines Road. The nurse there was pretty, and I winked at her. She didn't like it, and without fully understanding the nature of my ailment said I would do for Dr James O'Brian. Dr O'Brian, a lecherous-looking man of around fifty, suggested that I should see him in his surgery at Grangegorman Hospital. He listened sympathetically to my account of how I tossed about in bed each night and asked me to drink more stout. He also advised me to take glucose on toast before retiring to bed. I tried, but it didn't work.

'Well, we'll give you something that will work,' Dr O'Brian said with a smile full of confidence.

I was soon awaiting my turn in an anteroom of an impressive therapy hall. The talkative Irish maintained a grim silence here, though once in a while someone would remark to himself how much good the treatment had done him. I didn't know what the treatment was. I didn't even know what they did to me on the five occasions I reported for treatment. All I know was that they would give me an injection in the arm and ask me to count. I never counted beyond sixteen before falling asleep. When I got up, tea and biscuits were offered to me. It was only after the remedy had failed and the doctor had suggested I find a woman for myself I realised I had been given electric shocks.

Unable to sleep, I began to frequent dance halls. But I didn't care to dance. I liked the waltz music and the way people held each other—close and warm. Wish the whole world would come together like that and freeze. Then, then only would I get up and choose a partner for myself.

It was a 'woman's choice'. A girl—a couple of years older than I—came up and asked me to dance. She was nice but slightly large at the hips, though not as large as Elsa. I held her close to my body, and felt a stirring in my loins. Seeing her home, I kissed her on her lips and breasts. She didn't like it; she had to go to confession the next morning and hadn't yet finished the penance for her previous offence.

18

We would kiss and play. We would lie naked beside each other. But we did not have sex. She was too frightened of hell, and kept saying that God was watching us. Every time I had an erection she would say, 'God is watching you'. Though I didn't believe it, my penis always shrank at the mention of the Deity. We spent many evenings together, after she had put in her nine-to-five at Yvonne's Smoke Shop. She stole cigarettes by the carton for me and I smoked fifty a day. Though I don't smoke now, I am still interested in the subject of cancer. Cancer can be beaten.

We had a lot of fun. We took a trip to Cork together, for which the priest nailed her. The inevitable hour arrived: she had to choose between God and me, she told me. Never before had I faced such stiff competition. Julie left me, and I missed her a lot. I was lonely again, drinking and feeling sick every night. My monthly allowance wasn't enough for the life I was living in Dublin. I had thought of studying at Trinity College and had taken an appointment with the history professor. But I didn't go. I was tired of Dublin; I was tired of sitting whole days on the O'Connell Bridge counting the barges transporting stout from Guinness's Brewery. I was tired of College Green, Phoenix Park, St Stephen's Green, Grafton Street, Pearse Street, and all other streets.

I left Dublin one September morning. It was no different from the morning I had arrived. It was wet and miserable. And once again I was leaving nothing behind me.

6

I went to Leeds. My uncle, Kenneth, my father's younger brother, worked for an insurance company in Leeds, and that decided it. And there was also the university.

My uncle, and my aunt Judith, received me warmly in their semi-detached house on Chappeltown Road.

'Welcome home, Tristan,' said my uncle, with a hand-shake. 'You certainly look like your father.'

'He does, doesn't he?' confirmed Judith.

I felt instantly at home, the way I never did in India. My mother never said I looked like my father, and I am as dark as she. Sometimes I had felt I was not my father's son, when I saw Mother flirting with her friends. I would then go and gaze at my father's photograph on the mantelpiece and see that I had his broad forehead and thin lips.

I had my first good meal in months: roast beef with Yorkshire pudding. We retired to the living-room, and Uncle gave me one of his precious cigars. He offered me another the next day, but I told him I preferred my Wood-bines.

Uncle and Aunt talked a lot about Father. They felt it was a shame he died for India. 'If only we'd freed India in 1939, it would have been better for all,' said my aunt.

Uncle disagreed. The British should never have left India, he argued. Look at the mess the Indians have made, and now they are coming in shiploads to mess up life in England.

'We gave you a sound administration, roads, railways, justice, law and order. And all you gave yourselves were another 50 million mouths to feed, and now you ask us to feed them!'

I couldn't have agreed more with Uncle. But I didn't like

him referring to me in this way. It made me feel I was a part of the corruption the Indian Congress Party had set in motion. I was one of the family and I had come 'home' at last, though on an Indian passport. Given the time, I would be English; I was three-quarters English to begin with.

My aunt inquired casually about my mother and then dropped the subject. She asked if we owned a house in Delhi and whether I would go back after I had finished my studies. 'India needs educated people like you,' she remarked. 'And you will be able to find a suitable wife from your own community.'

I told her I had no wish to return to India, and as for a wife I could find one here. My uncle didn't appreciate that, and sermonised: 'You must not be like the other Indians, and if you take my advice, son, keep away from them. We've done all we can for India, and it is now up to you to bring progress to your country. As for mixed marriages, they don't work, and it is not simply a question of colour. Apart from colour there is a culture, and a lot of other things that go to make a community. I feel sorry for the Indians who come here, creating problems for themselves and for us. Look at the slums they have built! And the jobs they have taken from us! Why should they be porters and plumbers here when they could be administrators back home?'

I wanted to change the subject. And I felt it was impolite of me not to inquire about their life. I began, 'Well, Aunt, I know Uncle's age since he is two years younger than my father. That puts him at forty-six! How old are you?'

'Not as old as your uncle,' she said stiffly.

There was an embarrassing silence. I broke it.

'You have a nice house, Aunt. When did you buy it?'

'Five years ago.'

'How much did you pay for it?'

'We are still paying,' Uncle evaded the question. They obviously took little interest in themselves, I felt.

It seemed that the conversation for the evening had run out. And it was not past nine. I needed a drink. I told Uncle I wanted to go out for a stroll. He and Aunt readily agreed.

I entered a pub a block away and sat down by the bar. I

ordered a pint of bitter, and gulped it down. I felt much better and ordered another. A whore, around fifty, sitting beside me leaned over and asked if I had a match on me. From between her painted lips hung a crumpled cigarette. I lit her cigarette, and we got talking. I ordered more bitter for myself and for her. I don't remember all we talked about, but I do recall her saying that her father had been a cavalry officer in India.

'Closing time,' the barman called out. I ordered four more glasses of bitter. The whore and I drank it up fast.

'Come to my room, chuck,' she said.

'No, no.'

'Oh, come,' she insisted, pulling at my shirt sleeves.

'Please, no,' I pleaded.

She looked at me with sad eyes, and I noticed how ugly and dirty she was. I felt sorry for her and gave her a ten bob note.

'I am too old, I know,' she said. 'You are like my son. Come, I'll show you my daughter. You'll like her.'

'Some other day,' I replied, walking towards my uncle's house.

She followed me to the door. I beseeched her to go away. She agreed if I would let her kiss me. Just then Uncle opened the door and saw the whore's arms round my neck. He let me in without a word, and I straggled after him to my room in the basement.

'Breakfast at eight,' he announced.

'Goodnight,' I called out.

He left without responding.

I was up at six, shaved, dressed and ready for breakfast. In spite of all the beer I had consumed I slept badly during the first part of the night, and in the morning I found the bed too cold. I sat on the only chair in the room, looking at myself in the mirror on the dresser. I knew they would ask for an explanation, and I would tell them the truth—I felt sorry for her. But I wasn't concerned about what they thought of me: to them I was just another Indian and I had proved it. It would be difficult to explain the facts anyway: that I wasn't really an Indian—but his own brother's son. Did they realise that the Anglo-Indian community was their creation, which they discarded when they had no further use for it. And because we allowed ourselves to be used to keep their trains and their trams running, the Hindus suspected us of disloyalty. I belonged somewhere—even if I did not belong to them.

Uncle and Aunt maintained a discreet silence regarding the happenings of the previous night. I waited for them to speak up, ready with my explanation. But the conversation centred on what was good for breakfast, and I was twice asked to take an extra slice of bacon. When Uncle had left for work and I was getting ready to go and register at the university, Aunt contended that a mother cannot do the job of a father, that young folks need a father to inculcate in them a sense of morality and character.

At dinner, Uncle let drop that he had found a good home for me very near the university. The landlord and his wife were spiritualists, he said, and with my Indian bent of mind I should find myself in congenial surroundings. I would be allowed to cook for myself in my room, and on Sundays I could come over for dinner. But I must make sure to phone before I came. The next day my uncle and aunt drove me to 37 Clarendon Place.

'This is your room, ducky,' said the wiry old lady, leading me up three flights of narrow, creaking stairs into an oddly shaped room. 'Though it is an attic, it is the warmest room in the house . . . and the quietness is frightening,' and she shivered to prove her point. 'It is a blessing to a writer—a tenant of ours wrote a book here.'

'Was it published?' I asked.

'No,' said Mrs Dixon, 'it never was. His inspiration petered out and his funds vanished and he couldn't pay his rent. I and Dicky—my husband—did all we could to make him finish the book. But he disappeared one night and we never saw him again. Took his litter of papers along but left his shoes and clothes behind. It was a woman who did him in, I think. But here, let me show you the view from the window.'

It was the kind of view I had dreaded all my life. On the

23

horizon a hundred chimneys pierced the smoky, grey sky; nearer, there was a clutter of dirty terraced houses flanked by rows of dustbins. I pulled down the blind, swearing never to look out again.

'How much?' I asked.

'Thirty shillings a week. You will manage your meals.'

'Yes,' I said, taking out my wallet.

'Wait. I must tell you that the roof leaks from one corner and we can't afford to get it fixed. But I will give you a bucket to catch the water. Also, the room below you is a church. There's a meeting twice a week. Your uncle said it would do you good to attend the meetings.'

On Sunday, I stood suffocating in a small room crowded with bald men and ugly old females in formidable hats. They sang with such a deafening gusto, and so out of tune, that I couldn't make out a syllable. I had no choice but to act as if I were one of them. I joined in with 'Cockles and Mussels'.

When the fanfare ended, all, out of breath and tired, sat down. They closed their eyes. So did I. Then an old lady stood up in a trance. She swayed to the left and then to the right, and then back and forth. But she didn't fall. She steadied herself, and pointing a crooked finger towards the rotund figure of Mr Dixon, prophesied, 'I see a young man from a far-off country in your house today. He has in him that—that will bring you happiness and prosperity.'

All eyes turned towards me, and people came up and shook hands with me. A couple of crones blessed me with a kiss. Mr Dixon, brimming with delight, walked up to me in his slow, consequential strut and patted me on the back. 'You'll be very comfortable with us, mate,' he chuckled. 'You've come to a right respectable home.'

That night after supper, the Dixons asked me down to the kitchen and made a place for me by the fireside. They gave me plenty of tea to drink. But the next day it rained, and the roof leaked from three places instead of one as I had been assured earlier. I was given three buckets to catch the water. My complaint that the door had no bolt was attended to, and a large stone was brought into my room as a temporary measure to keep the door shut.

Had it not been for the Dixons' respectability I would have stayed there longer. The President of the India Association, who had somehow managed to get my name and address, came to see me. With him there was a white girl. Mr Dixon would not allow the girl to come up to my room. The President, Mr Rajeshwar Dayal, called Mr Dixon a racialist bastard and swore he would get in touch with the local M.P. The Dixons asked me to find another lodging as soon as possible.

A fortnight later I had found a room on Cromwell Road. It was a better room, with a sink in it. The sink proved most useful. I had by then met Jane, a Geology student. The most attractive thing about her was her long, tapering fingers. I used to kiss her hands; didn't like kissing her on the mouth for she had bad breath. She told me she suffered from chronic constipation. My friendship with Jane lasted a few weeks, but in those weeks she consumed a large number of tinned peaches. She loved peaches. She would gorge a two-pound tin at a sitting and then be sick. I didn't mind it: it made me feel tender towards her. But I didn't relish washing the sink out after she had vomited and collapsed on the chair.

I missed Jane when she left me for another man. I sent her the four tins of peaches that were left over by parcel post with this brief message: 'These tins bring painful memories of what I have lost.'

She wrote back thanking me, and saying I was the kindest man she had ever known.

7

No sooner had I settled down in my new place and begun
research on 'Henry II's Conquest of Ireland', than Mr
Rajeshwar Dayal paid me a second visit. He was again accompanied by a white woman, but a different one. Mr Dayal was
working for his Ph.D. in Sociology and had been in residence
at the university longer than any other Indian. This was his
last year—as far as the Graduate Committee was concerned.
He was dark, thick-set and balding, with blood-shot eyes
and an unusually large mouth. He pictured himself as another
Gandhi and had as long a record in fasting—though inter-
mittently. The girl with him, Gisella, had the fierce look of an
eagle, and yellow matted hair.

'As Benjamin Franklin said,' began Dayal, 'we must all
hang together, or else we shall all hang separately.' Gisella
gave me a sour look, and nodded.

'The India Association has been formed to safeguard
your vital interests, as I was saying last time, and as I say
this time. We have socials to get together at Dipwali,
Republic Day and on Independence Day. Our Association
welcomes all people irrespective of their caste, colour, conscience and creed. We represent all nationalities and minor-
ities, and we work for the protection of the coloured people
against white prejudices.'

Gisella again nodded assent. I asked what sort of prejudices one faces.

'Housing!' snarled Dayal. 'Seventy-seven per cent of
landladies won't take in Indians, do you know?'

'What can you do about that?'

'Do? We can do everything. We can boycott them. We
can form co-operatives. We can force the university to build

26

special residences for us.'

'What do the authorities feel about the Association?'

'First class! The Mayor is our worthy Patron, and the Vice-Chancellor is our Honorary Chairman. But we have to keep on our guard. Some of the professors are coloured-conscious. Do you know that only fifty per cent of the members of the Association failed their examinations last year, while seventy-five per cent of the non-members failed. The university is now finding it very difficult to fail active members of our Association. We have issued a solemn warning that if they fail us we shall appeal to the Human Rights Commission. If you want to pass, join the India Association. We will fight for you.'

I agreed to join the Association and paid my annual dues of fifteen shillings.

'We now welcome you to the India Association. But I must warn you that some "fifth element" has sneaked into us and is trying to wreck us from the inside. Even the Executive of the Association has been invaded by undesirable characters, and our respected Secretary has turned a turtle, and is impedimenting the smooth flow of our efforts to make a success of the Dipwali celebrations next month. I will send you a copy of my open letter. And you are invited tomorrow to a party I am giving for new members. Bring your girl and your bottle.'

I told Mr Dayal that I didn't have a girl, but I would bring a bottle.

'Gisella will arrange a girl for you. No life without woman in this country.'

Gisella looked me up and down as if she were sizing me up. She nodded assent, and the two left.

The President's open letter arrived by the morning post. I have preserved it, for a reply to this letter was circulated a few days later, which was wilfully ascribed to me and which cost me my membership in the Association.

Dear Member/Friend,
RE: DIPWALI DAY CELEBRATIONS
A mimeographed letter from our Secretary Mr Shituloo

Raman, addressed to me, is reportedly in circulation with a clearly malicious intent to stampede the smooth working of the Association and to create difficulties in the observance of the Dipwali festival in the Union building. *The Committee is in full command of the situation. All arrangements are in full swing and the function will be very definitely held according to the programme announced.*

Dipwali is a very auspicious day for the majority of our membership. Somebody has obviously chosen to 'cry wolf' just on the very eve of our celebrations. The members of the Association will not excuse the tantrums of any crackpot in their ranks—whatever his office in the Association may be. It would seem from a reading of the letter that somebody has planted in the Secretary's mind a very sneaky canard which has driven him to an apparent state of unreason. It would seem that the Secretary has been made to swallow an elephantine lie, which has choked all reason out of him. Some sinister monster is perhaps breathing hot and cold over his shoulders.

The Association's constitution is very clear about the duties of the various officers. Problems crop up when someone suddenly begins to succumb to that mortal itch to over-reach oneself. The Association has a solemn pledge to redeem. Now the President suddenly finds himself in an unenviable position of having to redeem fallen souls.

The Association is not in a mood to give in to counter-democratic forces masquerading in innocent disguise and swearing in the name of democracy by the mouthfuls and often with both ends of the mouth. Threat has no place in democracy.

There is a strict possibility that the Secretary's letter may have actually been written by someone else to discredit him. If so, the Secretary must speak out and clear his name. Anyone out to create mischief will be punished. The clear sunshine of truth, reason, service and democracy, will send the creatures of darkness back to where they properly belong. Threat and democracy are hardly compatible.

So, dear friends, come one and come all, rain or sunshine. Getting together occasionally contributes so much to our belonging together. I assure you, again, that I am in full control of the affairs of the Association.

With cordial greetings for the occasion, and always at your service,

Yours devotedly,
Rajeshwar Dayal,
PRESIDENT.

At first glance the President's letter did not appear strange to me. I felt he had a strong adversary in the Secretary, and the situation required strong measures. Besides, it was written in a style with which I was familiar, and I knew that Indian sentiments can best be expressed in Indian English. I should have read the letter more carefully and kept my mouth shut. I certainly should not have taken it to the party.

Mr Dayal occupied the front room on the ground floor of a dilapidated terrace house. There were eight other rooms, all occupied by Indians. The strong smell of spices assailed my nostrils as soon as I entered. Dayal received me warmly with a hug, and introduced me to several Indians and Pakistanis who were present. There were half a dozen girls as well—all whites. He asked Gisella to present my date to me. Gisella nodded, and brought a plump girl called Lydia, who walked with a limp. She had very heavy calves and thighs, with large varicose veins. When we sat down on the carpet, and I took a swig or two from my bottle (rum for a change) I could see her blue panties. They seemed to hold her sex together like a brassiere.

We got talking. I asked Lydia what brought her to join the India Association. She told me she was left pregnant by an English boy, who wouldn't pay for her abortion. Then she met her present boy-friend, Amul Bose—a waiter on the London–Leeds Pullman train—who got her money for abortion from the emergency fund of the India Association. Since then she had been loyal to the India Association and had not dated a white man.

I was beginning to respect the Indian community when Dayal tapped me on the shoulder and whispered that he would like to discuss something with me in private. As there were too many people in the room and in the hallway, he decided we should go to the lavatory. He locked the door after us so that no one would disturb us.

'Do you want to have Lydia as your girl?' asked Dayal.

I was taken aback. I didn't want to sound rude. I said, 'But isn't she Amul's girl-friend?'

'No. Amul Bose cannot satisfy her.'

'I don't quite understand.'

'As President of your Association, I look after every aspect of the members' welfare. You look to be a good man, and Lydia is a good girl.'

'But she told me she had an abortion—a white boy left her pregnant.'

'No. Let me tell you that it is not true. Amul made her pregnant, and as he could not pay for her abortion he appealed to me. To protect his reputation and not to set a precedent for paying for abortions, I gave out that she was pregnanted by a white man and then deserted. And that the India Association, which is free of class, colour, creed and conscience, helped a white woman against a Satanic white man. It helped to build our international image.'

'All the same you cannot call her a good girl,' I protested.

'Why not? What is wrong with sex? Besides, Amul did it orally—I mean manually—by hand.'

'I don't understand.'

'He put his sperms into her by hand. It can be done.'

I felt disgusted. I felt like walking out of the place immediately. But I had to be courteous to a host who was only trying to help me.

'You see, I have a girl in India. And I don't want a serious affair.'

Dayal laughed. 'Girl in India! *Yar* (friend), what has that got to do with enjoying life here? I have a wife in India. No life without a woman in this cold country, I repeat.'

'In that case I shall find my own,' I said.

'You won't find anything as good as Lydia,' he insisted.

'Perhaps not,' I said, opening the lavatory door. The pungent odour of spices was a relief after the smell in the lavatory. Dayal had been farting the while he was persuading me to accept Lydia.

When I returned to the room, Lydia was surrounded by four admirers, all talking to her at the same time and she being attentive to all. One was insisting that she try the *pakaros* (dumplings), made from lentils he brought with him from India and prepared to his mother's 'prescription'. Another, who occupied the attic of this house, was lamenting that owing to foreign exchange difficulties he could not take delivery of his Jaguar. The third regretted that he hadn't learnt cooking before he came to England, but then he had three cooks back home and would send for one. The fourth, who had been turned out of his flat for pissing on the street from his window, was gabbling about his magnificent garden in Patna. And all were vying with each other to teach Lydia Hindi, and she wanted them all.

I stood perplexed. Across the room, leaning against the wall, was an immaculately dressed Indian. He was small, wide-eyed and completely bald. His teeth were like fangs, and when he spoke he made a hissing sound. Every five minutes he would raise his head and put drops into his eyes from a green plastic bottle. He would then skip around like a hare and return to his place against the wall. Seeing me alone, he hopped up to me and introduced himself. His name was Santosh Kumar and he had just completed his Master's work at Leeds and was now proceeding to the Sorbonne to do his doctoral work on Marcel Proust.

'I am sorry you have lost Lydia,' he hissed.

'I don't care for her,' I retorted.

'Isn't this hilarious?'

'What?'

'The whole bloody thing! Did you see the President's open letter?'

'Yes, I have it on me.' And I dug into my pocket and pulled out the letter.

He read it out sonorously, in keeping with the style in which it was written. I now found it terribly funny and could not control my laughter. A couple of Indians, who were at loose ends, looked at the two of us with unconcealed curiosity and disapproval.

'One can write an excellent parody of this letter,' quipped Kumar.

'Why don't you do it?' I asked.

'I am leaving for Paris tomorrow, and I won't be here to enjoy it. Why don't you write it?'

'I don't think I could do a good job.'

'Try. I'll write it for you.'

I don't know what I said, but I am sure I did not ask him to write it for me and append my name to it. However, three days later I received a mimeographed copy of a letter, which read:

Revered President Dayal,

My whole heart ached from the bottom to see the demons of the India Association 'cry wolf' in your august presence preparatory to the most auspicious and holy of occasions—the Dipwali Day Celebrations. Your sacerdotal powers were for a while dimmed by these vultures of darkness, but the 'clear sunshine of truth, reason, service and democracy' of which you are a living embodiment will send these evil souls 'to where they actually belong'.

How right you are in saying that problems crop up when men and women 'succumb to that mortal itch'. India's population explosion is one facet of this immortal sin, but with you at the helm of affairs let no man scratch now. 'Some sinister monster is perhaps breathing hot and cold', but it will shrivel before the manifestation of your penetration, and run away like a dog with its tail between its legs. We are sure that you are 'in full control of the Association' and will not excuse 'the tantrums of any crackpot'. You will drive your sword of truth into the very bowels of the Association (be it elephantine) and make it move. Satan will flee for his life, and the angels of God will flutter their wings above you, and the Dove of Peace will perch on your shoulders and peck at your head for nourishment.

In this letter I have humbly tried to convey my warm

feelings towards you in the sublimity of style of which you are master.

I remain wedded to thy service,

Tristan Elliott.

The letter threw me into a panic. My first reaction was to go and see the President and tell him I had nothing to do with it, that somebody had played a dirty joke on him and used my name. But then it struck me that he would be furious at the moment and it might be best to let some time pass. Also, it would be better to pretend total ignorance about its existence and when told about it, to put up a good show of annoyance.

While on my way to the cafeteria, who should I meet but Dayal! He was in a rush, but stopped to say that he had read the letter and much appreciated the support I had given him. He wished other Indians would follow my example, so we could come together as one large family. He, however, pointed out that I had made one mistake: I had misunderstood 'mortal itch' for 'population explosion'. I stood dumb for a moment, then smiled and accepted the compliment. It seemed the natural thing to do.

In the evening the Secretary, Mr Shituloo Raman, a medical student, came to see me. He congratulated me on my 'brilliant satire', as he put it, and said that it would teach the old rogue Dayal his place in the Indian community. Shituloo was a dark, stout little man with a goatee. He wore unusually thick glasses which kept sliding down his nose and which he kept pushing up with his forefinger. He was in a terrible state of excitement and kept pacing up and down my room as he recalled what a hypocritical scoundrel Dayal was. I did not interrupt his monologue, nor did I deny the honour of having written the letter. Shituloo invited me to a curry dinner the next week.

'Do you like curry?'

I told him I did not enjoy curry, that I had ulcers and took no hot food.

'Without curry you will get nowhere in this country. Curry is the one thing that brings English and Indians together. Give a girl a hot curry, and then a mixture of sherry and cider to digest it. And she will run into your bed. Do you have a girl friend?'

'No. I have been here less than a month.'

'A month! I got my first girl the day I arrived. They like sleeping with Indians.'

'Why?'

'Because the Indians have greater retentive power. By the way I will give you some Ayurvedic birth control pills which I manufacture myself. It is hundred per cent safe. You don't give them to a woman—you take one yourself twenty minutes before intercourse. Wait, let me see if I have some for your noble self.'

He took out his wallet and gave me four pills.

'This is good for free sample. But remember you must take it twenty minutes before intercourse, and with distilled water. You can buy a bottle of distilled water at any chemist. And you can buy these pills from me at friendship discount price.'

Shituloo Raman patted me on the back and left.

Next afternoon there was a loud knocking on my door. Afraid it might disturb my landlady's afternoon nap, I rushed to open the door. Dayal and Gisella were there.

'Come in,' I said.

'What I have to say can be said from here,' barked Dayal. Gisella nodded.

'I offered you my hand of friendship, and you repay me with treachery. You write a most filthy "satire" and strengthen the hands of my enemies at a time when we are fighting for our very survival. And you accept an invitation to dinner from that Moloch Raman. You are worse than the British. At least we know that the British are our enemies and we can be on guard against them. But you are like the serpent in Eve . . .'

'I didn't write the letter, I swear.'

'Swear by what? Your mother or your father? Do you know who they are?'

'Come in,' I pleaded. 'I will tell you the whole truth.'

'We know the truth about you Anglo-Indians. You are all

34

traitors, blackguards, knaves and time-servers. If it were not for you people, we would have had *swaraj* (freedom) fifty years ago, and there would have been peace and prosperity in the land. But you, with two drops of British blood in you, sold us to the Imperialists. Remember, blood does not mix like water—and I shall see that you meet your Waterloo at my hands. The Association has no place for renegades in its constitution. Here, take your annual dues.'

And he threw a fistful of coins at me, and spat.

The two left. Gisella looked very fierce.

I went down on my knees and picked up the coins scattered around the door. It added up to twelve-and-six; some must have dropped in the cracks on the floor.

I went to the nearest pub and got stone drunk.

8

Early this morning the door bell rang. I answered, and found on the steps a dozen tins of sardines and a bottle of Médoc. Written on the bottle, in a neat hand, was: 'Take care— Marie'. I looked out and saw Marie at the end of the path where it meets the metalled road. She waved to me. I waved back, and beckoned her with my hands to come. She didn't. She walked backwards, still waving to me. If it hadn't been for the inherent danger of being recognised, I would have run down and fetched her.

Marie! I had almost forgotten you and my tins of sardines. It is a week since I last saw you. But I am glad you thought of me, my sweet little girl. Are you afraid that I might stretch you on the bed, naked, and kiss you from toe to head? I would, if I got the chance. And I am going to get you, Marie, do what you like. I am a one-eyed man! So what?

Yesterday was bad. My good eye burned and watered. I was frightened of going completely blind. How would I find my gun? It is true I keep it loaded in the far corner of the living-room, and I am never far from it. This is easy, for I spend most of the day and night in the living-room and the kitchen. And I have had some practice in reaching for my gun blindfolded. For instance, if I were to go blind sitting on my table, I would have to stand up, turn left, and walk straight six steps, and the gun would be in my hand. If I were to go blind in the kitchen, I would have to grope till I got to the door, then turn right and walk thirteen steps for the gun. I mustn't go blind in the bath, for I haven't worked out the directions yet. And then Elsa would get me. She would tuck a napkin under my chin and feed me along with the baby.

Porridge for both of us.

36

9

It is not the fear of going blind, for I have seen much and have no desire to see more. It is the fear of being left helpless, the fear of being doled out pity and charity, the fear of being compelled to live. To be for ever dependent on Elsa: to tell her age by feeling her sagging breasts, to tell my own from the calendar which others must read out to me. To follow the progress of my son's growth from the changes in his voice, to be given the description of the woman he is marrying, to sit in the pew and hear a hoarse voice pronounce: 'I now declare you man and wife.'

No, a brief obituary for me. 'A man of about thirty was found dead of a gunshot wound in Mountain View on Friday. No foul play is suspected. The R.C.M.P. are withholding his name until the next of kin are informed.'

Elsa can come and collect the dirty linen and throw it in the laundromat. She can have my wallet and my cheque book. But my letters and diary I must burn while I can see the flames. With this in mind, I emptied out my suitcase on the carpet and went through each paper carefully. Actually, I had destroyed a good many of my personal papers when I got married to Elsa and thought I was making a fresh start in life. But I had held on to two letters from Heather Malleson. One was written to me a few months before I was married, the other—a prophecy—I received about the time my son was born. It was addressed to me care of the Alumni Association of Leeds University of which I am a 'member in good standing'.

14 November 1967

Dear Tristan,

Your letter inspires—no spurs—me to write immediately (on receiving it!)

So destiny never closes her account!

Since you have told me this, then you yourself must have drank deep of this experience! Also, your God is one of dread and grim justice!

But enough of this preaching to one another about life. I am cut to the depth of my being, and very unhappy.

I am tired of facing regrets, reproaches, my own, and other people's unhappiness.

But enough of this as well.

I expect you have a thundering contempt for me. I can face it.

What you say is right and my agreeing does not infuriate me—it makes me love you!

Laugh at this and find it amusing!

Love from one for whom you have contempt!

But have you—deep within yourself?

No, you haven't. For some reason something softens this contempt. I miss you badly and deeply—this will satisfy you. I want you back!

Don't for a moment think you have been deceived! It is myself I keep deceiving right along. I go through endless moments of turmoil, and at times the host of different personalities within me get entwined in an utter state of confusion.

It is only to you I can say, 'Wherever I go or am, I am haunted by your presence'. At times I am seized with such fears because of this! Were I to tell this to anyone, they would think me insane!

I feel lost—I see no way out of this maze. Why is this so? Tristan, Tristan!

Is it too late? I will do anything!

Yes, what you say about me is right. Now I shall express my own opinion freely concerning *you*.

You are proud of your intelligence—in perceiving people's innermost thoughts. Extremely proud (perhaps to the point of conceit!)

And because of this people sometimes suffer unjustly on your behalf (myself excluded).

Why?

Because you are interested in proving yourself right, in satisfying this conceit. The hunger to gain this satisfaction suppresses consideration or kindness which you should have for the other person's feelings.

Also, people can do things for you: hundreds of things (big and small) to show their fondness for you—expressing it in their different ways. If, however, it doesn't happen to exactly suit you at the time, or if it isn't actually to your convenience at that time—then it is dispensed with.

And you have suffered from it! That you cannot deny!

To me, however, you have been both heroically kind and cuttingly cruel (this will appeal to your sense of the dramatic!)

I feel you have a grudge against the world—and against yourself. You must have had a very unhappy childhood. Also, I feel at times that you are not a normal person—from the things you do!

With reference to women you are—in a way—immature. You ask more from them than is good for *their* welfare (exclude me from this).

Of course, they have their choice. But the fact that you ask is selfish—a person who does this is *less*, not *more*, of a M A N—that is—less of a creature of reason and control. Not that I am exactly in a position to criticise you for this. Not I! (seriously).

I believe that the urge to be 'immoral' or 'unconventional' (choose a hundred alternative words for the same meaning) springs from a laziness of mind, and a lack of will to face the demands of life.

Both God and you know that I am not in a position to write this to you—because both of you know what I have done. (But God can see clearer than you—so remember your place!)

Now I will say why you do not hate me.

Because when you were selfish and cross-grained, I was kinder to you than anyone you had met before. I was consistently kind. I could be so, because I knew things could be no worse—I could trust in circumstances being better, but knew that they could not be worse.

39

When you were kind, I knew that things could be worse, i.e., revert back to the former.

Do you understand?

That is, it is easier to face things, however bad they may be at the time—when there is a promise of better things to come. But to face the possibility of circumstances turning back on one again—that is worse. I believed there was this possibility, for you are temperamental, vain, and contemptuous of others. But I will admit that you keep to your own general broad principles in the long run. But general broad principles skim over circumstances in the short run.

As a result of everything (from beginning to end) you know me better than anyone else. You can hurt me more than anyone else! You also know this.

I know you well (to the extent that I can tell what you are likely to do under a given set of conditions). What you have *done*, I don't know. I don't want to.

This letter is more than you had bargained for, but not totally unexpected.

In the usual woman-like fashion I have written far too much, pages of nonsense—to be folded and put in one of those drawers and perhaps looked at later with some kind of feeling (hard though this may be).

But I believe that, as a result of this, we know one another better, i.e., to the absolute extent.

What happens, as a result, depends on (if anything) the choice made.

God will know, even if you don't want to, that this was written under stress and therefore must be sincere. He will also understand why this appears to be so nonsensical and badly written. He will also know what you will think, on receiving this, although I may never find out. And He will, I trust, forgive me, though you may not.

Heather

God did not forgive her. Christ did not forgive her though he had said, 'Her sins, which are many, are forgiven; for she loved much'. Here is the other letter, written after she had married a Syrian, and was divorced.

To Tristan Elliott

WARNING

You are to turn to God in Jesus Christ and commit your life to Him. The alternative is that you may die suddenly. I was given the gift of prophecy when I converted and became a Christian in March 1970—when I was born in Christ. I was given the gift of prophecy as written in Acts, Ch. 2, verses 17–21 inclusive. To *check* this you may contact:

> Dr Gerald Mitchell,
> Consulting Psychiatrist,
> King James Hospital,
> Cardiff, Wales.

I am set as 'watchman' as written in the Old Testament, Ezekiel, Ch. 33, verses 7–8.

Verse 7. 'So thou, Son of Man, I have set thee a watchman unto the house of Israel; therefore thou shalt hear the word from my mouth and warn them from me.'

Verse 8. 'When I say unto the wicked, O wicked man, thou shalt surely die; if thou *dost not* speak to warn the wicked from his way, that wicked man shall die in his iniquity; but his blood will I require at thine hand.'

You are to bring others to the Christian religion; you are to warn adulterers, fornicators, drug addicts, prostitutes, of death which may be sudden if they *don't* turn to Christ. You are to set up *other* 'watchmen' for moral laws and order—you are to 'fish' or bring in man for Christ. MOVE AND OBEY, *or* you might die suddenly and be answerable to God who *does* exist.

> Yours faithfully,
> Heather Malleson (Miss)

I met Heather at a Students' Union dance one Saturday. I can't dance, I don't enjoy dancing, but that evening I was feeling lonely and wanted company. I asked the prettiest girls around to dance with me and they all, some eight of them, refused. I was on the point of retiring to my flat when I allowed myself one last try. It turned out to be Heather. She didn't look striking the day I met her, and now I don't think she really was a pretty girl. But for nearly two years she was everything to me, and I haven't yet completely forgotten her. She had a broad forehead, large, wide and deep-set eyes with straight eyebrows, a thin nose expanding at the nostrils, thin lips, and a well-formed chin. Her blond hair was shoulder-length and fell in locks. It was her hair that first drew my attention, and during the very first dance I told her how I admired it. When I saw her the next day, she was bobbed.

'Why did you do that?' I asked.

She shrugged her shoulders and with a nervous laugh said, 'I guess because you liked it.'

It must have been my third dance with Heather when an English boy came up and tapped her on the shoulder. She excused herself, and left me standing in the midst of a hundred waltzing couples. I was moving to one side when Heather reappeared, and we began dancing again. She looked depressed, and I felt concerned.

'What is the matter?' I asked, pressing my cheek to hers.

'Nothing,' she whispered.

'There must be something. You look so sad.'

'I am not.' And she drew her body close to mine, and I could hear her heart-beat.

'Tell me,' I implored. 'Don't you trust me?'

'I don't even know you.'

'You will come to know me. Tell me.'

'You are a very persistent person. Well, he, Michael, called me to say he won't be seeing me any more. Does that . . .' She did not complete the sentence.

There was nothing I could say. I held her tight and kissed her several times on the side of her neck. She remained passive. The music stopped.

'Let's go and have a drink,' I said.

Holding hands, we went to the Union pub in the basement of the building. It was crowded as usual, and we couldn't find a table. So we stood leaning against a pillar, sipping cider. She didn't speak much, and I concluded that she was still thinking of the English boy who had left her.

We left the pub at midnight. Heather had a room on the second floor of an old house, a few streets from where I lived. I asked her if I could walk her home. She agreed. On the way we decided to meet for lunch the next day at the main entrance to the cafeteria. When we reached her place, she did not ask me in. But she kissed me passionately and I responded fiercely.

On returning to my flat, it struck me as rather odd that we had not asked each other's names, nor who we were and what we were studying. We had danced, drunk, kissed and parted.

10

In the days that followed, I got closer to Heather than I had been to any other woman. We would meet every day for lunch, and most evenings. We would go to a double feature film and sit in the last row holding hands, or kissing. Kissing mostly. Our hands wandered, and we would both get excited. Often, after the movies, Heather would come to my room and I would make her a cup of coffee. I would undress her, ritualistically, one garment after another. And I would kiss her, as I used to kiss Nellie: from toe to head. At times I would be reminded of Nellie and would suddenly stop or move away. She would be puzzled at my behaviour and ask me why I behaved so. She suspected that there was something in my past which made me act the way I did. I had assured her there was nothing in my past, that she was the only girl I had ever loved. It was a lie, but then I had made a good start on a lie. It was easy to live up to it, too, for I became very fond of Heather and soon convinced myself that she was the only woman I had loved.

I feel now that I should have told Heather the truth about myself. I should have told her about Nellie. I should have told her the facts about my background: that I was an Anglo-Indian—a race for which neither the English nor the Indians had any use. I had told her I was a Eurasian, which sounded better than being half Indian and half English. But Indians had a bad reputation in England, and I feared that even the three-fourths English blood in me wasn't sufficient to wipe off the stain of the one-fourth Indian. It was a mistake to have concealed anything from Heather. She was all love when I met her; she was all sex when I left her. Towards the end of our relationship, when she lied to me and deceived me and cheated me, I felt that some grim justice was being dealt to me. For it was I who had lied and cheated her in the first place. If at the end of our relationship I came out cleaner in Elsa's eyes, it was the beginning of another affliction. Clean or dirty, I was broken, and though my words had a deep impact on Heather, to me they often sounded hollow. Heather went mad because, in spite of her promiscuity, she was basically honest; I was, comparatively, more faithful to her, but less honest. And I was saved to the extent I was dishonest.

One bright morning, Heather and I went to York—her home town. She wanted to pick up some of her biology texts (she was studying for her Honours in biology), and I was keen on seeing the Minster. Her sister and her parents had gone for a week's holiday to Cornwall, and I had little difficulty in persuading her that we should spend the night in her two-bedroom home. I was to use her father's pyjamas and to sleep in her sister's room.

We decided on a feast. I went to the nearest grocery store and bought some mushrooms, minced beef, and a large bottle of Merrydown cider. When I got back Heather was going into the bath, closing the door after her.

'Can I come in?' I asked, casually, knowing she would refuse.

To my surprise she agreed and opened the door. I sat on the toilet seat like a good boy, and watched her strip herself naked.

She reached for the soap.

'Let me help you,' I said, and took the soap from her hand. I began applying it to her body in a workman-like manner, going about my job with the disinterestedness of a nurse bathing an old patient. But when it came to drying her with a towel, and the thick, brown pubic hair stood out clean and fragrant, I lost control. I knelt down, and covered her sex with kisses. Millions of them.

We cooked the meal together. I am expert at frying mushrooms.

As we both were tired, we retired to bed early. I went into her sister's room, and she into her parents'. I had every intention of sleeping alone, but the mattress springs were digging into my sides. After tossing in the bed for about an hour, I called out to Heather to find me another mattress. She came to my room and turned over the old mattress, but the other side was no better.

'Let me sleep with you,' I said. 'After all we are so close to each other, anyway.'

'It is too much of a risk,' she replied.

'Not really! If we make up our minds we needn't do it.'

'But have we made up our minds?'

'I have. Besides, I am pretty useless after drinks. And you know how much I've taken.'

I got into bed with her and immediately had a half erection.

'Heather, let's do it. We belong to each other.'

'Do we?'

'I do. Unless you have someone else.'

'I have never had sex.'

'You don't have to lie.'

'I swear.'

'I believe you. It makes you all the lovelier.'

'Have you any condoms?'

'I have something better,' I said. And I got up and fished out from my wallet the four Ayurvedic birth control pills that Shituloo Raman had presented me. I took two of the pills to make doubly sure there would be no risk.

I got into bed with her.

'Now we must wait for twenty minutes,' I said. As I kept peering at my watch, I began to lose my half erection. I did everything to stimulate myself, and asked Heather to help me. But nothing could bring it back to life. I felt terribly let down. Heather showed great understanding and put down my failure to nervousness, drink, and a good conscience. I thanked her, clung to her like a child, and went into a sound sleep.

When I woke at sunrise, I had the erection for which I had worked so hard at night and which was long overdue. Afraid I might be betrayed again, I pushed it into her quickly and without the least formality. She was in no mood to make

46

love, but she understood my predicament and did not resist. It worked. Before we left for Leeds by the ten o'clock bus, I had done it three times. I felt happy and proud of myself: as proud as Henry II must have felt after putting down the barons.

The next three weeks were full of joy and happiness. Our passions, wild and boundless, mingled in complete sexual satisfaction.

For three weeks we reached out to an insouciance where we both felt calm and assured. Her little breasts grew firmer, the nipples harder, her sex opened up like a chalice. I used to cover it with my hand, and call it 'my handful of love'.

For three weeks the world stood still. There was neither hate, nor misery, nor pain. Heather was beautiful, I was beautiful, all things were beautiful.

At the end of the three weeks Heather told me that she had missed her period. Except for the night at York we had taken no risks—I had spent more on condoms than on my meals.

I was frightened. 'It will come,' I said without much faith. 'It might just have been delayed.'

'I hope so,' Heather replied.

'Don't worry. I will stand by you. We'll get an abortion.'

'Never. I will never go in for that.'

'But why?'

'I will not take the life of my own child.'

'There is no life in it yet,' I said, half in anger and half in fear. 'It would be worse than murder to bring a bastard into the world.'

'He has a father,' retorted Heather, looking me straight in the eyes. 'Never suggest abortion to me. You don't have to take him if you don't want him.'

'Try and understand me, Heather,' I pleaded. 'This is not the time to be sentimental. Neither of us can take on the responsibility of a child. Nor did we want a child. It is an accident. Let's go and see a doctor—and be rid of it. The sooner the better.'

'Stop it,' she shouted.

I put my hand on her shoulder to comfort her, but she

47

brushed it aside. Then she ran out of my room. I called after her, but she kept running. Awkwardly, clumsily, as women do.

The illusion was over. Nothing was beautiful. I was going to be a father, and Heather a mother. I did not think of the unborn child, but ruminated on the sort of life I would have with Heather. Thirty years together! Love each other, comfort each other, talk to each other. For thirty years?

Love seemed to have frozen with the changed circumstances, neither could comfort the other. What use was there for words?

There remained the possibility that her menses might have been delayed. Shituloo Raman was the man who could relieve me of my fears. I sought him out. He was squatting on the floor in the middle of his room pounding some herbs in a mortar, which he held between the soles of his feet. Around him were scores of bottles with crudely printed labels on them, which read: *Ayurvedic Birth Control Pills for Gentlemen Only. Money Refunded if Proved Otherwise. Made from Ancient Indian Herbs. Expiry Date . . . Price . . .* (Raman filled in the expiry date and price by hand at the time of selling, varying them according to his customers' abilities to pay and his own skill at persuading them.)

'Come in,' said Raman cheerfully. 'Take your seat, please.' And he pointed towards the bed.

'Don't you like having a chair in your room?'

'No,' he replied with a lascivious glint in his eyes. 'If you want girls then don't have chairs in room. Once there is a chair, they never get up. Make them sit on the bed—it is easier. Well, dear friend, what can I do for you?'

'Shituloo, tell me how safe are your pills?'

'Hundred and one per cent safe.'

'You see, I tried your pills out. Took two of them, and I think the girl is pregnant.'

'My dear friend, you are a fast worker. But don't worry, it is not your responsibility.'

'It is my responsibility. I don't want to marry her and I don't want a child. Do you understand me?'

'How do you know it is your child? And you can't have

a child if you took the pills as prescribed.'

'Shituloo, I took the pills five hours before intercourse. And I didn't have distilled water.'

'Ah, my friend, you don't follow the medical advice and then you blame the doctor. Twenty minutes before time, I told you, only twenty minutes before time. Why did you take five hours overtime?'

'I didn't. It's this way. After I took the pills I lost erection. It came back after five hours.'

Shituloo Raman laughed himself hoarse. 'Ha, ha, ha, ha. My friend, don't disgrace the Indian community here. I will present you some pills for erection.'

'I don't want your pills,' I said angrily. 'What am I to do now? I don't want a baby.'

'That is easy. Say it is not yours.'

'How can I say that when I know it is mine.'

'Well, good sir, how do you know it is yours? How do you know it is not somebody else's?'

'Because she was a virgin when I met her.'

'How old is she?'

'About twenty.'

This time Shituloo rolled over on his side with laughter, upturning the mortar which he held between his feet. The herbs lay scattered on the dirty floor. He swept them into a heap with a hairbrush and put them back into the mortar.

'Look what you have done, friend!' he said, pointing towards the herbs. And then, waxing philosophic, he began: 'There are no virgins in Leeds. Here the girls get fucked before they are twelve years old. This is England, my friend, not India. Women here don't have the modesty of our Indian ladies!'

'Shituloo, you must help me. And you must help me to help her. She must not have the baby.'

'Get her to take it out. I am a doctor, you know, and I will do it for you at friendship discount price.'

'How much will that be?'

'Can you afford ten pounds?' And he looked at me with cunning to see how much I was prepared to pay.

'Yes. But she doesn't want an abortion. She won't agree

49

to an abortion.'

'You leave that to me. Let a doctor talk to his patient. You bring her here and I will discuss her problems with her.'

I surveyed the filthy room. Herbs, bottles, clothes lying on the bed, several pairs of slippers and sandals all over the floor. Where would Heather sit? There was no chair in the room.

'Why don't you come over to my place tomorrow evening? She will be there.'

'O.K. But one thing, friend. I must talk to her alone, that is, not in your esteemed presence. You understand why?'

'Yes, you may talk to her alone. But you mustn't tell her that I suggested an abortion. Convince her in your own way of the need for an abortion.'

'Right ho! I will come tomorrow at seven o'clock.' And he picked up the pestle and began pounding the herbs.

I fetched Heather to my room at about six. She looked very tired, perhaps from lack of sleep. I sat near her, gently kissing her hands and lips. I told her that a doctor friend of mine would be visiting me and that she should talk the matter over with him. She said that she would rather talk to her own physician. I persuaded her that there was no harm in taking two opinions, that the question of an abortion did not arise for we were not even sure why she had missed her period. Reluctantly she agreed to talk to my friend.

Punctually at seven, the door-bell rang. Shituloo Raman was there.

'Come in, Dr Raman, come in,' I called out aloud so as to prepare Heather for his entry.

Dr Shituloo Raman was dressed nattily in a three-piece blue worsted suit with thick white stripes. He wore bright red nylon socks which still had the gold label price tags on them, and light brown loafers. From his coat pocket emerged half of his stethoscope, and in his hands he held a cheap, plastic raincoat.

I introduced Dr Raman to Heather as a very dear friend and an experienced surgeon. I then withdrew from the room with the excuse that I must run down to the store and get some wine and cheese.

Instead of half an hour I stayed away for an hour, knowing that doctors usually take longer than they say. I walked up and down the street, praying that all should go well.

At eight I returned.

Heather was lying on the bed, sobbing jerkily into the pillow. Dr Raman was not in the room.

'What's the matter, Heather? Where's the doctor?'

'Tristan,' she cried, 'why must you do this to me? If you don't want me, tell me to go. I swear I will never trouble you again. But . . . but don't do this to me.'

'I don't understand. What have I done? Are you all right?'

'Yes, I am all right,' she said, turning suddenly fierce. 'I could never have thought that you would try to palm me off on another man.'

'Are you mad? What are you talking about? Where is Raman?'

'Your dear friend left quickly enough when I told him I would slap his face . . . that I couldn't marry him—not even for the sake of my child. I told him that he was a swine. I told him that you too were a swine—that I would stay here, in this room, just long enough to tell you that to your face. Now that I have told you, I am going.'

And she stood up to leave.

'Sit down, Heather. I must know what has happened,' I said.

'Nothing, my dear Tristan, nothing. Now please get out of my way and let me go.'

'You may go, Heather, for ever and for ever. But not till I know the whole truth.'

I led her to the chair. 'Tell me everything.'

'Your friend told me that you have been pestering him to induce me to agree to an abortion . . . that in principle he is against taking a life. Did you ask him to perform an abortion?'

'Continue, Heather.'

'You first answer my question.'

'There will be time enough to answer. Finish your story

first,' I said, trying to control my temper.

'He said you were an Anglo-Indian—a class with loose morals, despised by all respectable Indians. That if I had any sense I should have nothing to do with you . . .'

'And what else?'

'He proposed to me. . . . He said he was prepared to marry me and to support me and my child.'

'Did you . . . ?'

'Of course not. But he kept insisting. He caught my hand and dragged me to the bed. He then tried to put his hand . . . I can't, I can't go on.' And she covered her face with her hands and wept hysterically.

I let her weep. When she had quietened down a little, I went up to her and wiped her tears with my fingers.

'Heather, how much of this do you believe?'

'I don't know. Sometimes everything.'

'I did suggest to him that he should persuade you to have an abortion. Rather it was he who suggested the abortion, and wanted to see you alone. I will kill him, the swine. Heather, you may go now.'

Heather went pale and stared at me with half-opened lips. Then she said, 'No, leave him alone. Promise you will say nothing to him.'

'I will kill the swine,' I reiterated.

'No, promise me. Stay with me. I want to be with you—always.'

I sat down at Heather's feet and buried my face in her lap.

11

I was afraid, and depressed. I didn't want to be a father. I would go down on my knees whenever I found a chance—in my room or in the gents at the university—and pray to God to save me. I swore to Him that I would never again sleep with a woman outside of marriage if he would only save me this one time. I stopped making love to Heather, for I rarely had an erection and my penis looked pretty decrepit most of the time. The idea of spending a life-time with Heather chilled me, and on reflection I found, that apart from sex, there was very little in common between us. She had rarely said an intelligent thing, took no pride in my researches on Henry II, was not interested in any news from outside Yorkshire, laughed at the wrong moments and had virtually no sense of humour.

But I was resolved on shouldering my responsibilities towards my child. I would acknowledge him as my son, pay for his maintenance, send him to Cambridge, and make a real man out of him. At times I feared he might take after his mother and lack my intelligence. That would be a shame. Instead of studying history or philosophy he might, like his mother, go in for biology and waste his life poring over microbes in a laboratory. That would be awful. And that would certainly happen—for fate seemed against me. Even my studies were not going satisfactorily.

My supervisor, Dr Geoffrey Adams, failed to appreciate the first chapter I had submitted. 'Not only is there not one, single original idea,' he complained, 'but even the rehash of others' opinions makes no sense'. Rajeshwar Dayal was perhaps right: these professors were prejudiced against the Indians.

After she missed her period, I had stopped seeing Heather in the afternoons. In the evenings I saw her as frequently as I used to, but had cut down on the movies. She was still very affectionate and I continued to undress her, but not as ritualistically. Instead of kissing her from toe to head, I used to put my head on her belly and pretend to sleep. In fact I was all the while trying to find out if I could hear the baby groan. With my ear to her belly I would pick up various sounds and vibrations and try to analyse them. Most of the time I heard a rumbling noise and knew it could not be the baby. I would often slip my finger into her vagina to see if I could spot a drop of blood.

One day, a drop of blood was on my forefinger.

'Look Heather! You are bleeding,' I said.

Heather parted her legs, examined herself in my presence, and cried out in joy: 'It's my period! Oh darling, it has come.'

'Darling,' I exclaimed. And we clasped each other. Then I knelt down on the bed and thanked God for His mercy.

But soon doubts began to assail me. 'Heather, are you sure it is your period?'

'Of course.'

'How do you know?'

'Well, Tristan, oughtn't I to know?'

I had been told that menses smelled of decayed vegetables. I put my finger to my nose. It smelt of faeces.

It was an awful shock. I had never thought my lovely Heather could smell so horrid, that 'my handful of love' could emit such putrid odours.

'Do all women smell like that?' I asked.

'I don't go about smelling people,' she exploded.

'Nor do I,' I said, taking umbrage at her tone. I could now take the offensive: it was all up with the baby.

Things returned to normal. I got over the baby and the offensive smell. It was good to be with Heather in the evenings, to make love to her, to hear her declare that she could never give herself to anybody but me. I became more confident of myself: Heather indeed was mine, and I needn't give her all my time. I could study for a change.

One Wednesday, Heather suggested that we should go to a charity ball the next day at the Students' Union. She did it after we had had sex, and that made the difference. I told her that I would rather stay home and read, and that she should go alone. She was reluctant, but I argued that we should not stick together all the time but try and meet new people—broaden our horizons through an exchange of ideas.

I did my stint of work on Thursday, but by nine I was tired. I decided to go to the British Council reading-room to scan the papers. It was here that I met Elsa Harbaur. She was an *au pair*, looking after the children of a Jewish doctor and studying English. She came from Munich and she loved England. 'The English are so frank and nice people,' she said, wriggling on her buttocks.

I don't want to describe Elsa. She was big and strong when I first met her; she is bigger and stronger now. She had morals then, and she has morals now. She has resisted the advances of many of my esteemed colleagues, though for the life of me I can't understand why they want her. I think Canadians want excitement and in a big way, like their neighbours to the South. And Elsa was big. I know of a rotund little Canadian—he is now in Mexico—who liked pinching the bottoms of faculty wives. Thank God he didn't pinch Elsa's—with one fart she would have thrown him off balance.

When Elsa stood up to leave for her home in Roundhay Park, I accompanied her to the bus-stop. As she didn't mind my holding her hand, I thought I might as well make the next move. As I brought my mouth close to hers, she caught me unawares and gave me a push that landed me full on my back. She was terribly concerned and helped me to my feet, repeating all the while, 'I didn't mean it'. I took this to imply that she wanted me to kiss her and so I tried again. This time she explained: no kissing on the first day. I appreciated that—you don't hear it too often. I arranged to see her again. As she had only one day off a week, we decided to meet next Thursday for a movie.

After seeing Elsa settle down imposingly on the top of a double-decker, I went to the Union to seek out Heather. The floor was swarming with couples, and I couldn't find her. So I went to have a drink in the pub downstairs. No sooner had I entered than I saw Heather. And with her the sleazy bastard Shituloo Raman. He had his arm round her waist and they were both laughing.

I was furious. I don't think I have ever been so enraged. My first impulse was to knock the goatee down, but better sense prevailed. Looking back, I wish I had given Shituloo a good hiding, for then his friends would have beaten me up and rid me of my love for Heather. Nothing releases one better from love than a sound hiding—I can say that from personal experience. I have a tooth missing: it was knocked out by the father of a girl I once dated in Delhi. And I hated the girl after that.

I felt that if I stayed a moment longer I might do something insane, and to do the sane thing would cost me five pounds. I could hardly afford the expense on my meagre allowance of thirty pounds a month, but it had to be done. I ran to the railway station and bought a return ticket to London, and jumped on to the train just as it was dragging itself out. My plans were to keep away from Leeds for a few hours, and after having reviewed the entire situation to talk coolly and calmly to Heather.

It was a long night. It was a long, dank night. As I sat alone in the dimly lit coach, things fell into their proper perspective. I had only got what I had deserved. I should have known better. I should never have had sex after I had promised to the Lord God—when Heather missed her period. I could hardly appeal to Him now for His sympathy or help. But self-accusations aside, she had deceived me. I could now see clearly why she had made me promise not to say a word to Shituloo after he proposed to her that evening at my place. Perhaps he had already slept with her, for wasn't Heather on the bed when I returned with the cheese and wine? And if he hadn't that evening, he would certainly do so tonight. I could see Shituloo swallowing his pills with distilled water, then pacing up and down his room for twenty minutes, pantless, in his red socks, with an erection. And then. . .

I could not bear the thought. I could not bear the idea of anybody, anything, going near 'my handful of love'. Mine, all mine, since I had deflowered it, opened it, loved it, kissed it. Tears came to my eyes and I looked out of the window so as not to be observed. 'It hurts; Oh, my God, how it hurts,' I said loudly enough to hear my own voice. And then I wiped my tears and became absolutely calm. I could see I had histrionic talent. I would wring Heather's heart as soon as I got back. I was dying to get back.

At eight in the morning, I was pacing the floor of Heather's room. She was in her nightie, sitting up on the bed and gaping at me.

'What brought you here?' she asked.

'Love of you, my dear,' I said with a forced smile.

She guessed there was something on my mind. She could guess my mind rightly; so could Elsa. But that's no reason for marrying.

'Well, how was the evening?' I began. 'I went to the Union at about eleven, but you weren't there. So I dropped in here. But you weren't here either.'

She did not reply, but looked at me in an attempt to ferret out how much I knew.

'Well, Heather, how did you spend the evening?' I asked again.

'I was at the dance, but left early.'

'How early, Heather?'

'About eleven.'

'A little later, perhaps,' I interjected. And I came and sat down on the bed beside her and began stroking her knees.

'Heather, you are a very pretty girl, and I love you. Do you love me?'

'Yes, of course I do.' And she snuggled up to me.

'Fine. Now let us get back to my question. What did you do last evening?'

'I told you I went to the dance.'

'With whom?'

Heather turned ashen, she began to shiver. So there was as much to it as I had thought.

'With a friend,' she said in a last frantic bid to cover up

her tracks.

'A friend?' I shouted. 'You call that pig a friend? A peddler of pills! Now I know why you didn't want me to kill that swine. Where did you go after the dance?'

'Nowhere. He dropped me home.'

'Liar. He took you to his room. I was following you, you didn't know that. He took you to the pub, and from there to his room. Am I right?'

Trapped, she became a little aggressive. 'If you know— why do you ask?'

'Because I don't know what he did with you in his room? Now tell me what he did with you, or I will go and kill him.'

'I swear, nothing. I just had coffee. I was feeling very sleepy.'

'And so you slept there?'

'That's not true. I was back in my room by one.'

'You weren't.'

'I was.'

'All right, you were back. But what did you do while you were there?'

'That is none of your business,' she hurled defiantly.

I had been expecting her to say that all the while. 'It is my business. Who else's is it? I—I who loved you, gave you my whole being, never for a moment thought about myself . . . Was even willing to shoulder my responsibilities towards the child. . . . I . . . I, and you tell me it is none of my business.'

'Don't tell me about your sense of responsibility. You— you looked bleached when I told you I had missed my period.'

'And don't you try and hide behind the façade that I have failed you. Tell me, what did you do? Tell me or I will go and wring his neck.'

'Nothing. We did nothing.'

'Did he kiss you?'

Heather burst into tears.

'Tears won't help you. Answer my question: did he kiss you?'

'Yes, he did.'

'And what more?'

'Don't. Please don't.'

'He touched you there. Took your hand and put it on his . . .'

'Stop it, please.'

'No, not now. We must get to the end of it, even if it breaks me.'

'Oh, my God,' she wept bitterly.

'You slept with him?'

'No, I didn't. I swear I didn't. He asked me . . . but I didn't. I swear.'

'To go with that beast! To open yourself up to him! To that dirty, filthy swine. Heather, I now leave you to him. All to him. Go to him. You will never see me again. Never.'

And I stalked out of the room. I felt another chapter of my life had come to a close.

For two days I could not eat or sleep. I could not sit still for a moment. I could think of nothing but Heather. Was it Heather's fault that she went with Shituloo? I kept asking myself. I introduced her to Shituloo; I encouraged her to go to the dance. Once with Shituloo, what could she do? And she may not have slept with him? And what about myself? Would I not have slept with Elsa if I had the chance? But she didn't know about Elsa. I had no right to blame her. I, too, was guilty. As guilty as she.

But it wasn't the guilt that sent me back to Heather on the third day. It was simply that I couldn't live without her. She was my breath, my body, my soul. I had no existence apart from her. 'My handful of love' was calling me, her tiny nipples were staring at me, her pubic hair was reaching out to me with all its fragrance.

> There has fallen a splendid tear
> From the passion-flower at the gate.
> She is coming, my dove, my dear;
> She is coming, my life, my fate.

I ran with all my might. Breathless, I stood in her room. With tears running down my face, I fell at her feet. I kissed her hands, her feet, her eyes, her lips, her neck, her throat.

I kissed her all over in a mad orgy of love and lust.

'Go wherever you want, take whomever you want, but don't leave me. Heather, that is my dying wish, don't leave me.'

She held me close to her body, her arms tightening round me. 'My boy! My poor, poor, boy,' she moaned.

12

I have never panicked the way I did today. I have never been so frightened. But I am glad it is all over. My good eye is as good as ever. But I must never again take unnecessary risks. To walk to the grocery store with a gun would invite suspicion, but better a gun than a white stick.

I went down to the store this morning. I wanted to buy some food and to see Marie.

'Thank you for the wine,' I said.

'What wine?' she asked, from behind the counter.

'And the sardines. But why didn't you wait?'

'I don't understand . . . there is some mistake.'

'You don't remember me?'

'No, I've never seen you before.'

'Are you sure?'

'Yes, I think so.'

I stumbled. I placed the order, paid the bill, and hastened back home. I put the barrel of the gun into my mouth and pushed it as far back as it would go. I should have applied some lubricant to it for it irritated my throat and set me coughing. I was still coughing when the grocer arrived with the parcel. He introduced himself as John.

I asked him in. He would be the last man to hear my voice on earth. I wondered what he would tell the police. But I was glad I had called him in. If it weren't for him, I'd be dead now.

'Here is the balance from your twenty dollars,' he said, handing me six dollars and a few cents. 'My daughter said you rushed out without waiting for the change.'

'You have a lovely daughter,' I said.

'They are both good girls.'

'You have two daughters?'

'Twins.'

'Ah, I have seen one—Marie.'

'You have met both. Marion took your order today.'

'No, it was Marie.'

John laughed. 'Marie is in Vancouver. It was Marion—they look alike, dress alike. . . .'

'You mean they *look* alike?'

'You couldn't tell the difference if you had to.'

I made John a cup of coffee. While he was sipping it, I peered into his face to check my vision. I could see the stubble of his day-old beard, the pores on his pug-nose, the capillaries in the whites of his eyes.

'There was a man sent from God, whose name was John,' I said.

'What?' he asked.

I did not refer him to his Bible, but picked up the gun from the table and put it in its rightful place in the far corner of the room. I saw John to the door.

Marie, why did you go away without telling me? And when are you coming back? I am so lonely here. From my window I can see the fall leaves—mostly yellow, but not the yellow of the skirt you wore the first day. The sky is clear and endless. The unending earth stretches out to meet it. It meets, perhaps, where you are standing. On the waterfront.

13

It was drizzling the first of the many Thursdays I went out with Elsa to the movies. I had my umbrella, and Elsa had forgotten her raincoat. That brought us close together: I put my arm round her and drew her near to shelter her. I wanted to kiss her, but the roads were slippery and my back still ached from the fall I had had the previous Thursday. I think I did a good job of fending off the rain: when we reached the cinema, only the right half of Elsa was drenched.

We didn't sit in the back row. Elsa was always on guard and she chose a place in the middle of the hall. But there were not more than fifty people present and that afforded us some privacy. I took Elsa's hand in my own. There was a lot of flesh on it, but it was limp. Still, it was the beginning, and who knew what opportunities the screen might present? I had chosen a war film, *Paths of Glory*, in the hope that there might be a tense moment in it when I could reasonably be expected to lose control of myself.

It came earlier than expected. A French battalion got caught between its own artillery and the enemy fire. I dropped Elsa's hand, leaned forward to give the impression that I was spellbound by what was taking place—and waited. As the guns boomed and the blood spurted and the men sprawled dying, I gave a quick gasp and caught Elsa's hand and put it on my lap. 'No,' she yelled, and hastily pulled away her hand. A dozen heads turned towards us. I pretended as if nothing had happened—that I was still under the spell of the horror I had witnessed. Elsa could argue it out —if she wished to—that it was the brutal killing that had brought forth the cry from her. We never talked about it, not even after we were married. Often I thought about it, but didn't know what to say or ask.

After the show we went to a café. Elsa does not smoke or drink. She has no vices, she is the biggest piece of virtue I have known. She talked about her family: her mother who owned a toy shop, and her two brothers and a sister who were studying in Munich. Her father had been a Nazi officer during the war and had been killed in an ambush near Amsterdam. She talked about the Jewish family she was staying with and how good they were to her now. But they hadn't taken kindly to her when she first arrived, because of her father. And she didn't know much English. One day she broke some crockery, and her mistress cried out, 'Oh, my dear!' Elsa retired to her room and wept. 'What's the matter?' asked her mistress. Elsa replied between sobs, 'I am sorry to break the cups, but you shouldn't have called me an animal.' And the mistress explained the difference between 'dear' and 'deer'. But such misunderstandings were few, for Elsa had a facility for learning languages. She wanted me to take her to India after we got married so that she could learn Hindi.

She asked me questions about my family. I told her my father was English, hoping that it would bring me closer to her for she had much admiration for the English. I also said I had an uncle in the city who had given me up for lost after my spiritualist landlord threw me out of his house. There wasn't much I could tell her about my mother, and Nellie was too sacred to speak about. I found Elsa's questions tedious, but it struck me that no other girl I went out with had cared to know anything about me or my family. All they wanted to know was when I would take them out again. A few wanted to know if I had other girl friends.

Elsa never inquired about other girls. She was the only girl who took some interest in my studies. I told her I was writing a thesis on Henry II. She had not heard of Henry II and asked why I was not working on Henry VIII about whom she had heard her mistress talk. She wanted to know what precisely I was doing on Henry II. This provided me with an opportunity to recall all that I had read since my arrival in Leeds. And I was once again reminded of how little work

I had done and of my professor's comment on my first chapter. She, however, thought I knew a lot and that one day I would be a professor myself. I laughed. But at that time I did not know of a country where there were more professors than janitors.

The talk about my researches put me in a bad mood. So that when Elsa suggested it was time for her to leave, I was glad. At the bus-stop I kissed her. It was a rushed one, and with her permission. I kissed her many times afterwards—in the cinema and outside—but always with her permission. It was safer. And it was mostly a clean, brief affair. No licking or spitting into each other's mouth. Sex was out of the question. 'No sex outside marriage,' Elsa had declared. And what Elsa said she meant.

After Elsa's bus jogged out, I went to Heather's apartment. She did not know I had been to see another girl. After the Shituloo episode we had promised to remain faithful to each other. At the same time she had agreed to my suggestion that we should meet and go out with other people as well—to fulfil the purpose of a university education. I was relieved, for at that time I had already made a date with Elsa and was afraid Heather might find out. Not to have sex with anybody else was the key point. And it suited me well, for Elsa did not attract me sexually. Besides, I was fully satisfied with Heather.

Heather was sitting in a chair, reading. I lay down on her bed and beckoned her with my hand to come and lie down beside me. I undressed her without uttering a word. My first words to her that evening were, 'Let's make love.'

'All right,' she said, perfunctorily.

'You don't feel like it?' I asked.

'Not really.'

'Then we needn't do it.'

'No, let's do it, if you want to.'

'But I can wait.'

'No. You want it now. I'm yours—all yours. You can have me whenever you want. You don't have to ask me.'

Soon we were rolled into one, pulsing, throbbing, giving

and receiving. I felt I belonged to Heather, as I belonged to no other woman. I felt her power over me, the power of the flesh: potent, earthy, immediate. If I have to meet my God, let it be through Heather and not through His Commandments.

14

Months slipped by—tortured, restless months. I tried to break away from Heather, knowing her full power over me. But I failed. Can the Ethiopian change his skin, or the leopard his spots?

I tried hard, and many times over. I had begun seeing her only at weekends and encouraging her to go out with other men. I particularly wanted her to go out with Shituloo Raman and even spoke well of him. If only she would go out with Shituloo, the disgust would kill my love for her.

But I held on to the weekends. I convinced myself I needed them, not for the gratification of my own urges, but as a divining-rod to fathom out where she stood in relation to other men. No man who took her seriously would leave the weekends to her, and as soon as she told me she could not see me at weekends, I should know that the man had arrived.

Looking back, it appears that the week-days sufficed for Heather.

But I must not be unfair to Heather. Though she was promiscuous, selfish and unreliable, she was capable of immense love. And not with her body only. When I was ill for two weeks, she nursed me more affectionately than my mother ever did. She was with me morning, evening, and night for those two weeks: feeding me, watching over me, giving me company. Not once did she date during my period of illness, even though I begged her to go out for an evening.

It was soon after I got well that I proposed marriage to her. She had spent the evening with Michael—the boy who had told her he would not be seeing her any more the day I met her.

She accepted my offer.

'Think it over carefully,' I said.

'I don't need to, Tristan. I have loved you since the day I met you. I have been waiting for you to ask me.'

'I want you to think it over, Heather. Marriage is no small matter.'

Heather laughed. 'Chickening out? You didn't think I would say yes, did you?'

She was right. I had not thought she would accept me that readily and leave me no room to manoeuvre. And what I was now asking her to consider were actually my own fears.

'Not at all. But you must try and probe into the future, weigh everything coolly, for once you are in there is no escape. Think not in terms of days, but years. Thirty years, forty years together, perhaps more. Not simply sex, but companionship; a home, and children—and I their father. I am going away for a fortnight to give you time to think. I should not be here to influence you while you are making up your mind.'

'But I know my mind,' asserted Heather. 'And what about this going? Where are you going?'

'Apart from providing you an opportunity to decide, I have some journals to look up in Dublin and London. I must finish my bloody work—I still have three chapters to write.'

'Well, then, you are really going for work!'

'Not altogether. I too would like to think it over . . . not my proposal, but how best we could set about it. *If* we get married, where would you like to live?'

'*If?*'

'Heather, Heather!' And I smothered her with kisses. 'I shall marry you, come what may.'

I had planned on making the best use of my trip. I saw my supervisor the morning of my departure. He asked me if I had thought out what work I wished to accomplish in Dublin and London. I answered in the affirmative. My first task was to map out Henry II's itinerary in Ireland. Mr Eyton's *Household and Itinerary of Henry II* might need emendation, and the movements of the restless king from day to day might require verification. I had also to establish the authenticity of 'The Bull *Laudabiliter*' of which Henry made such good use. My professor commended my goal, but doubted my ability to improve on Eyton. He wished me the very best of luck and a happy voyage.

Early next morning I was at the National Library on Kildare Street. My briefcase was stuffed with note paper and index cards, and I had a most impressive bibliography. But half the books I wanted weren't in the library, and those that I did find had little to do with my topic. I spent the day turning over the pages of journals and by the evening had managed to consult some thirty volumes. I had also taken down two pages of quotations (these my supervisor deleted from the final draft of my thesis). The next day was better: by the time I left the library I felt I might run out of index cards. But I didn't. The following two days I stayed in bed with a cold, and when I recovered it was obvious to me that I had enough material to write a Master's thesis. I had given up the idea of correcting Eyton's itinerary of Henry II, and the Archbishop of Dublin refused to meet me to discuss 'The Bull *Laudabiliter*'. He did, however, send a priest who invited me to attend Mass on Sunday.

The question which weighed most heavily on my mind was marriage to Heather. Did I really love her? Or was it merely the flesh that I had mistaken for love? She satisfied my entire being, every pore of my body. But with what? That remained to be answered. If it was plain sex, then it would be unwise to marry Heather. And only by making love to another woman could I find out my true feelings for Heather. I thought of Julie at Yvonne's Smoke Shop. Though I had failed in the past, I could try again.

Julie received me warmly and presented me with a packet of cigarettes and a bar of chocolate.

'Listen, Julie. As soon as you can make it come over to my hotel. We'll have a snack and then go to the Ritz. *South Pacific* is a delightful film.'

Julie looked disturbed. 'I can't come to your hotel!'

'Why not?'

'Because . . . because I don't know how ye'll behave.'

'God! Telling me that after knowing me all these months, and I a better Christian . . .'

'Since when?'

'Since the hour the Blessed Virgin herself came down the chimney of my room and I all the while reading *The Book of Genesis.*'

'Alone?'

'Of course.'

'You lie. I don't believe you.'

'Why?'

'Because she'd be too frightened to come to your room alone,' said Julie, moving away to attend to the other customers.

This was a bitter blow and needed to be washed down with stout. On my way to the pub I ran into Robert. He was from Belfast, studying law at Trinity. I had met him when I first arrived in Dublin. We picked on O'Connors.

We'd both had four pints each. Around us a heated discussion was going on. All were agreed that Ulster should be a part of Eire, yet everyone was snarling at everyone else. Suddenly Robert bawled at them: 'What you want is a boot in your arse. Why the hell should the North join you when you can't even look after your patchy South?'

'Be God!' gasped one in anguish. 'Looka dhat fella sayin' we can't look afther ah'selves an' he a chiseller from school!'

'North!' shouted Robert, jumping off his stool and throwing himself into the middle of the group. 'I'll give you the North for breakfast tomorrow if one of you can name the six counties ye are fighting for.'

'Armagh, Derry, Tyrone . . .' came voices from different corners of the room.

'That's only three!' I said.

I wish I hadn't. Someone threw a bottle of stout which caught me on the back of my head. Blood dripped down my neck; I was rushed to the nearest dispensary. An hour later I was walking back to my hotel with an ugly bandage round my head.

The next day I left for London, two days ahead of schedule. I did less work in London than I had done in Dublin.

Though I went to the British Museum every day, most of the time I couldn't find a seat. I spent the mornings queuing up for coffee in the cafeteria in the basement, thinking of Heather. I had to make love to someone to find out how genuine my feelings were for Heather. The bandage round my head made me somewhat unpresentable, and when I removed it I found that two inches of my scalp had been shaved off. I bought myself a fez.

I didn't know where to find a woman. I tried the Speakers' Corner at Hyde Park. I had heard a lot about it.

The first speaker I approached stood on a garden chair. He was dressed like a clergyman, except that he wore a bus conductor's cap. 'It's ten years now,' he said, 'that I have been trying to establish the sex of God. Not till I discover the sex of God can you call yourselves the children of God. You are all children of men—men like me!'

A thin, sharp voice from the crowd silenced him. 'Oh, no! You aren't a man.'

The speaker smiled. 'Will the person come forward?' he asked.

All eyes turned as a young girl stepped out, holding a half-eaten apple.

'Tempt me not with that forbidden fruit, my dear,' he said, as the audience roared with laughter. I pushed my way through the crowd to get a better view of the whore. She was awful, God help her.

A little way off stood a stiff-necked, middle-aged Salvation Army officer conducting a hymn sung by a choir of six beautiful girls. As I stood admiring them sing,

> *O God of my Salvation hear,*
> *And help a sinner to draw near*
> *With boldness to thy throne of Grace,*

I realised how difficult the road to heaven was. And how gladly I would follow them to the other place.

The next speaker I stood to listen to was a small Irishman in a black coat and sky-blue trousers. 'Any more questions before I go for me breakfast!' he asked.

'Yup,' said a voice from the crowd. 'Did you ever have a woman in your life?'

'Yes,' said the speaker, climbing on to a soapbox. 'I had one las' night. I was dhressed in me blue suit and was lookin' very han'some. Afther I had me dinner, I found that I'd with me a pound note left. I took a taxi and off to Piccadilly I was and there I saw the mos' beautiful girl standin'. She said I was a fine man and she'd come with me and so we went to her place. She gave me whisky and a hamburger, and we stayed together the whole night. In the mornin' I get up to go when she says, "What about some money, dear?" "No darlin'," says I. "I'll take no money from ye afther all ye've done for me." At which point she started shoutin' . . .'

I didn't wait for him to finish his story. I took the tube to Piccadilly Circus. There were many women on the street, some of them were pretty. I approached one who reminded me of Elsa. But she refused—she didn't sleep with Asians. I must say this for England: it may be a country of shop-keepers, but the people are not without principles. And you get what you pay for, neither more nor less. This I discovered when I found the girl I wanted. Her name was Lily.

She had a sweet, innocent face. She was tiny, with thin arms and legs, and no breasts. But she had shapely hips. I agreed to pay her five pounds, and she directed me to a nearby hotel. The room would cost me a pound.

The desk-clerk wanted to see my passport. I told him I didn't have it on me.

'In that case it will be two pounds, sir,' he said.

I turned to Lily. She shrugged her shoulders as if it were none of her business. I paid the two pounds.

The room was small and dark, with no windows. The bedsheets were clean, but there was no pillow. In a corner stood a jar full of water and an enamel basin. There was nothing else in the room. Not even a towel.

Lily lit a cigarette and stripped herself from the waist down. She lay down on the bed and asked me to come over. I came and sat beside her.

'Take off all your clothes,' I said.

'Why?' she asked.

72

'Well . . .' I didn't know what to say. 'Put out that cigarette,' I added.

'Why?'

'So that I might kiss you.'

'You don't have to kiss me.'

'Are we going to make love?'

'Go ahead. Don't waste your time. You've only got half an hour.'

'Yes,' I said. And after a moment: 'I can't while you are smoking.'

'I don't see why you can't. I don't mind your smoking, if you want to.'

I took off my pants. She lay there puffing smoke bubbles. I didn't have an erection, and I didn't know what to do. I looked at her sex, it was buried in a mass of dark brown hair. I squeezed it with my hand, saying, 'My handful of love.'

She burst out laughing. I began to shiver; the room was not heated. And I knew I wouldn't be able to do it.

'I can't till you take that cigarette out of your mouth,' I said angrily.

'Bad luck to you,' she retorted.

'I have paid you for it.'

'There is no refund,' she answered.

I reached for my pants. While I was getting into them she said, 'All you Indians are strange. You want too much for your money, and you finish up getting nothing. I once had a bloke who kept mumbling "Hey Ram, hey Ram" the while he was trying to get his little screw in. He couldn't; he burst into tears and fled. There was another, a Pakistani I think, who fucked himself on this very bed. He did it thrice in the half hour and then fainted—fut. I threw that jug of water on him to get him back on his feet.'

I left. The next evening I left for Leeds. Instead of the fortnight, I had been away for only ten days. But much had been accomplished. I was now sure of my feelings for Heather. She was indeed my life, my soul. In the train I kept humming my last words to her, 'I shall marry you, come what may.'

15

Close to nine I reached Heather's flat. From the street I could see that the lights of her second-floor flat were on. I rang the door bell. She did not answer. I rang again. There was no response. I knocked at the door, hard. Still she did not answer. I stepped back on to the street, from where I could see a section of the room. I got fleeting glimpses of Heather —and a man. I came back to the door and again pressed the door-bell button. She did not come down to let me in. Was the bell out of order? I could deceive myself no more. I squatted on the steps, waiting for the man to leave. Every few minutes I pressed the button. I was sweating profusely.

At eleven the lights in her room went out. I was in utter darkness, and in communion with God. I knelt down and prayed: 'My God, my God, why hast thou forsaken me? why art thou so far from helping me, and from the words of my roaring?' I heard His voice, clear and metallic: 'For I the Lord thy God am a jealous God, and visit the sins of the fathers upon the children unto the third and fourth generation of them that hate me.' 'My punishment is greater than I can bear,' I cried. The voice of God was silent.

A policeman on the beat stopped by and asked me what I was doing. Waiting for a friend, I answered. An hour later I was asked the same question. Forgotten my keys, I said. He reminded me what I had said earlier. He took me to the police station, but did not lock me up. He was kind. He left me in the company of two other policemen who gave me tea and crumpets. At five they let me go.

I was back on Heather's door-step, pressing the door-bell button. I sat down; the morning chill was creeping into my bones. I wasn't thinking. It seemed that I had lost the capacity to think, to feel, to be hurt. I felt like a dog who had been locked out by mistake.

At six, the door opened and a huge man walked out. He wore a scarf which partly concealed his face. But I noticed he had small eyes, a long hooked nose and very thick lips. He was darker than I.

Five minutes later I rang the bell again. Heather came down in her nightie and let me in. She was pale and dishevelled.

'What are you doing here?' she asked faintly.

I fell down and kissed her feet. I was weeping, I could not control my tears—they came faster than I could wipe them away.

I followed her to her room. She got into her bed, and I sat in a chair. I kept staring at her, trying to hold back my tears. I felt choked. I couldn't speak.

Five minutes or more must have passed.

Heather's eyes grew moist and she began sobbing. That did it.

I could not trust my voice. And so I acted. I walked up to Heather, slowly and deliberately, and with one jerk ripped the nightie off her back. She did not utter a sound, but clutched at the blankets. I wrestled them from her and threw them into the sink and turned on the tap. She tried to cover herself with the pillow and the sheets, but they too went into the sink. She moved towards her wardrobe, but I threw her on to the bed. She sat there, naked, huddled like a lost child. Neither of us said a word.

At last she spoke, 'What do you want?'

'The truth,' I said.

She did not reply. She buried her face in her hands and wept.

'We have had enough weeping, Heather, you and I. This is not the Day of Judgement, yet something must be decided today. Do you hear me? Come, tell me everything.'

'What do you want to know?'

'Who was this man in your room last night?'

Heather began as if she were going to tell me, but stopped.

'Go on,' I said, softly. 'But don't tell me he is just a friend.'

'No, I won't tell you that.'

'Say something. Don't sit there quiet, and don't be afraid of me.'

'I am afraid of you—I am.'

'No, you are not afraid of me. You have made a covenant with hell.'

'I don't understand.'

'You will. But go on . . . tell me who was this man?'

'He is a student at the university.'

'An Egyptian?'

'No, a Syrian.'

'Well, continue. What is his name?'

'Moustafa Sadat.'

'When did you meet him?'

'Only today. I was having lunch when he came and joined me, and we began talking. He invited me for an oriental dish and then he came to drop me home. I asked him in for coffee.'

'And then?'

Heather hesitated, faltered, and I knew she was conjuring up a lie. I smiled—a butcher's smile—and asked, 'First tell me about the oriental dish. What's it like?'

She fell for the diversion. 'It's called *kababs*; it's hot, I didn't like it.'

'Not as good as my mushrooms?' I said. 'Do you remember how I fried mushrooms for you in York! Wasn't that a lovely feast?'

Heather looked puzzled. She peered at me to see what I was getting at. Did she think I was letting her off the hook?

'I liked the mushrooms,' she said, unconvincingly.

'Good. Well, you then asked him in for coffee. No harm in that! But why did he stay here all night?'

'He forgot his keys.'

Unaware, like a reflex act, I slapped her on the face. She started howling. I dragged her from the bed and threw her on the floor. I pinned her to the floor with the weight of my body and covered her mouth with my hand. 'Whore! I too forgot my keys last night. A cop picked me up from your steps and took me to the police station. While you were making love with that animal—that squint-eyed elephant! My God, where have you led me to? There is no mercy in you, and all my prayers are in vain. How long will it last, Lord, how long?'

My fury was soon spent. I got up, and so did Heather. She sat on the bed looking at me with frightened eyes. I spoke to her gently, 'Heather, I will not hurt you. I will not abuse you. I will not shout, or rant, or curse you. All that is over. Forgive me for what I have done. But tell me the truth, even though I know it. You have nothing to lose now, Heather.'

'All right,' she said.

'Did you make love with him?'

'Yes.'

'And with Shituloo Raman—the day he took you home after the dance?'

'Yes, but not that day.'

'That doesn't matter. And with Michael?'

'Yes.'

'And how many more?'

'No one else, I promise you.'

'Me, Heather, me! You are forgetting me! You are forgetting the man who grovelled like a dog at your feet. One more question, Heather. You will answer it?'

'I'll try.'

'Tell me what sort of penises do these people have? I mean the size, the circumference, the colour? . . .'

'You disgust me.'

'Even you? It is good, for not the truth but the disgust shall make us free. To forget you, I must learn to hate you. I wanted to marry you—I came back early to tell you that I was now ready to marry you . . . that you are the only thing I have in this world. But I forgot . . .'

There were tears again in Heather's eyes. Not the tears that fan themselves into tiny rivulets on the cheeks, but tears that grow on the eyes, magnify the eyes, till you see nothing but the eyes. Then they drop—like quicksilver.

'Forgive me, Tristan,' she said with bated breath.

77

'Heather, there is no forgiveness in this world, for there is no honesty. There is only God's grim justice. I shall go now. I shall go softly all my years in the bitterness of my soul.'

'You won't leave me?'

'I shall write to you and I shall come and see you. But I must go now.'

16

On reaching my flat, I felt calm and rested. There was now no option but to pull myself together. I wrote a letter to Heather—rather a long one. I don't remember what I wrote but her reply of 14th November gives some clue as to what I might have said. I did not close the doors completely on Heather. After the happenings of the previous night I felt assured that I could sever my relationship with her at any time of my own choosing. When I married Elsa four months later, I believed I had finally freed myself from Heather. In both instances I was wrong. Tragically wrong. But I don't regret it: I am the plaything of Fate.

At the core of my being, there is a strain of insincerity. Heather knew this when she wrote: 'To me, however, you have been both heroically kind and cuttingly cruel (this will appeal to your sense of the dramatic!)' This insincerity is really the rational part of me—the one factor which saves me from going the way that Heather did. My doctor has often asked me to see a psychiatrist, and it is the only medical advice I have always scoffed at. I am sane. A good proof of my sanity is that though I am ready to die, I have not yet killed myself. And when I do it, it won't be an unpremeditated act; it will be studied, prepared, regal, like Cleopatra's death. No hanging, no drowning, no jumping off roof-tops for me. Life is a stage, and veteran actors use guns. And I am both: actor and dramatist. I am, however, not a stage director, and my costumes are ready-made.

I returned to Heather as a dog returns to his vomit. But don't forget, a dog doesn't enjoy eating his vomit. He swallows only a little for medicinal purposes—to clean his system. And so with me: I used Heather the same way. I knew there was a close parallel between me and a dog, and on one occasion I behaved exactly like a dog.

I went to see Heather with my fez on. When she answered the door, I barked: 'Wow, wow.' Then on all fours I climbed the stairs after her. When we got into her room, I yelped and bayed. She didn't understand. Then with my teeth I tugged at her panties till I pulled them off. With my paws I laid her on the floor, and pow-wowed around her, sniffing, licking, yapping and howling. Then I fucked her. After it was over, I barked loudly several times, and with my tongue hanging out I pranced out on all fours.

Heather laughed herself into fits. However, the great symbolic meaning of my act was incomprehensible to her. She was not intelligent—not fit to be my wife.

I had been seeing more of Elsa since the previous summer. Her mistress occasionally allowed her an afternoon a week off as well, and Elsa and I would go for long walks. Over the Yorkshire dales and meadows, and along the railway tracks. Elsa loved flowers and trees and she knew the name of every herb or plant that dared to sprout. 'That's a Dog Rose, this is a Cowslip, that's a Dandelion . . . Bell-Flower . . . Dead Nettle . . . Autumn Crocus . . . Bulrush . . . Tufted Vetch . . . Crab Apple . . . Yellow Pimpernel . . . Willow . . . Birch . . . Beech . . . Oak . . .' Her list seemed endless. I only knew and cared for one flower, the Rose, and that too because of Blake's poem. I asked Elsa if I could have her rose. She gave me a confused look. I should have asked, 'May I have your cabbage?'

Elsa looked good at times. Especially when the sun was shining and she had on a light summer dress. I thought she would look better still under the vast Indian skies and land-scapes. She appeared a little too big for the small, fenced English fields. Sometimes like a Herefordshire cow.

I proposed to her one wet February afternoon in a barn in the Yorkshire Wolds. She accepted me. I did not ask her to think it over. You don't do such things with Elsa.

It happened this way.

We took the train to the Wolds. It wasn't wet or foggy when we started. It seemed an unusually warm morning for February, and I wanted to walk. Had the whole day to spend, and Elsa with me.

We hadn't walked for long when the wind rose and the rain came down. It was sudden. The sun was lost in the whirling clouds about us, and the rain-drops pattered on us. We ran into a barn.

It was empty, and dark. When our eyes got used to the darkness, we found the place damp. But there was some dry lumber piled in tiers. Elsa suggested we sit down and eat the sandwiches she had packed.

It was cold.

'I am cold, Elsa,' I said.

'It is cold here,' she answered.

'Come near me. Let me feel the warmth of your body,' I said earnestly. Perhaps honestly, too.

She moved closer, and I put my arm round her. I bent and kissed her under the chin, and down the neck as far as her dress would allow. She did not mind. With the back of my fingers I teased the nipples of her breast.

'Don't,' she moaned, looking at me with beseeching eyes.

I was surprised. I had always expected Elsa to command, to react swiftly and strongly. I couldn't imagine her pleading. I withdrew my hand.

'Elsa, will you tell me something?'

'What?'

'Before I ask, I must tell you something. It's just curiosity —this my asking you. I—I don't want to exploit you. I say this so that you might speak freely. I have known you . . . and not really, for I don't know why . . .'

I searched for the right words to frame my question. I felt embarrassed to ask what I wanted. Besides, the quizzical look on her face didn't help.

'What do you want to know?' she asked.

'This, Elsa,' I said with some hesitation. 'Why are you so afraid of the human body?'

'I am not afraid.'

'But you are afraid of sex!'

'No. Why do you say that?'

'Well, your notion that one shouldn't have sex outside of marriage. Is it prudery or fear?'

Elsa did not reply. Instead she began scrutinising the palms of her hands as if she were reading her fate.

'Let me put the question to you more positively. Have you ever had sex?'

'Yes, certainly,' she said, looking up at me.

'Certainly? And yet you keep pushing me away!'

'I cared for him,' said Elsa, softly.

I stood up. I sat down. I found myself dumb. It had never occurred to me to find out if Elsa cared for me or not. And it struck me that Elsa's feelings had never been my concern: I sought her out when I was lonely and wanted company. I had never asked Elsa if she needed me, if I could be of any use to her.

'I understand, Elsa,' I stammered after a while. 'It is my fault that you do not care for me.'

'But I do,' she said, pressing my hand.

It was the first time Elsa had touched me of her own accord. We always held hands, but at my initiative.

I didn't want Elsa to be sentimental about me. I felt very guilty, being reminded of my selfishness. I didn't want to know that Elsa cared for me.

'Tell me about this boy,' I said.

'What do you want to know?'

'Everything. Start from the beginning—with his name.'

'No, Tristan.'

'Yes, Elsa.'

'All right. Wilhelm and I grew up together. He was something like you, but a little fairer. His hair was dark like yours. We had known each other for nine years. He was both father and lover to me and we were making plans to get married . . .'

'What did he do for a living?' I interrupted.

'He was in his final year at the university. He wanted to be a dentist.'

Elsa stopped. I begged her to continue.

'We used to go hunting together. One day he had a bet with me that he would kill a boar with the first shot of a small rifle he had bought to kill rabbits. He was a good shot and I didn't doubt him, but I took on the bet to please him. We roamed through the forest for many hours, and got tired. I was leaning against the trunk of a tree and picking out the grass from my trousers when I heard a shot. I didn't look up to see what he had fired at. I didn't see the animal. I heard a cry, and saw Wilhelm rolling on the ground in agony. A wounded boar had charged at him and knocked him over. It had gored him between his legs.'

'Was he badly hurt?' I asked.

Elsa broke down, but quickly regained her composure. She did not shed a tear as she narrated the rest of her gruesome story.

'I shouted for help. I ran in circles around him, for I could not leave him alone. I had to be within hearing range of his cry as I called out for help. For three hours the forest rang with our cries, but there was nobody to hear us. My throat went dry and my voice froze until there was only his wailing left. I thought he would die and I wanted to be near him. I came and sat down beside him and began to blow cold breath on his forehead. At last a hunter came by. He and I got Wilhelm into his car. I shall never forget the drive. I sat in the back with his head in my lap. He was not bleeding much, but he was in terrible pain. By the time we reached the hospital he had fainted. I was glad he had fainted; I couldn't bear to see him suffer.

'He was in hospital for six weeks. I stayed with him most of the time. As he lay recuperating in bed, we talked about our future—our marriage. When he came out, he was different. He was a different man. He did not want to marry me.'

'But why?' I asked.

'Don't ask me any more questions, Tristan. I have told you enough.'

'Tell me the whole thing. You can't stop now.'

'If you want to know. He had lost his sex. He tried again and again, but it wouldn't work. O God, it was awful ... it was horrible to see him torture himself. I told him that it did not matter, that my love for him was not based on sex ... that sex was not important. But I couldn't make him

83

see. He would . . . he would try all sorts of things, ways, but it was useless. He underwent two operations, but the doctors couldn't help him. He was drifting away from me . . . I could see he was trying to break away from me, and I was afraid. I wanted Wilhelm—just as he was. I told him so . . . I told him we could adopt children, that I loved him . . . wanted to grow old and wither with him. It was no good . . . I couldn't convince him of my love. I tried very hard, Tristan, I tried very hard . . .'

'Where's he now?'

'Elsa pulled her hand away from mine. She looked at the sodden earth at her feet and continued as if in a reverie.

'I used to go to his place every day. One day he was unusually cheerful. "I am all right now," he said. "I can do it, you know!" There was something frightening about his cheerfulness. We lay down. He tried as usual. He began panting, there were large beads of perspiration on his face and forehead. "Don't tire yourself," I said. He laughed. It was a weird laugh like the howl of a beast. From under the mattress he pulled out the gun—the same gun he had used on the boar. Before I knew what he was doing, he blew out his brains. I took his head once again in my lap, but . . . but this time I did not have to call out for help.'

'Oh God, have mercy!' I gasped in spite of myself.

Elsa smiled sadly. It wasn't really a smile at all. But there is no other way to describe it.

'He would have lived, if I had been able to make him see that love and sex are two very different things. Anyway, you now have my story.'

'You think he would have lived if he hadn't experienced sex?' I asked. I felt sorry for her, and yet I couldn't associate this big woman with tragedy.

'I am very sure he would have,' she answered.

'I am not so sure,' I said. 'Perhaps he might have lived, I can't say. Sex is, after all, an important part of life.'

'I know all that,' said Elsa irritably. 'But Wilhelm mistook it for the whole life.'

'Then you should not blame yourself for what happened. You know, I too had an experience. It was very different

84

from yours. There was a girl called Nellie, in India, whom I loved. Like you, we thought of getting married, but we had never had sex. I mean real sex. She lost her legs in an accident. And then she would not have me. When I went to see her she pushed me away.'

'Why did she do that?'

'One can only guess,' I said. 'Between us there was a rhythm, a pattern of life, which endeared us to one another. When she was crippled she saw this pattern, this rhythm, destroyed. It wasn't true, though this is how she felt. She thought I could never accept her again.'

'Do you think you would have accepted her?'

'Elsa, that was one question I was spared. And today, sitting with you in this barn, I see more than I ever did before. Nellie may not have wanted me to face that decision. And you know why? Because she loved me. It is strange, but Nellie and Wilhelm were alike in some ways. Misfortune had placed them in another world and they didn't want our sympathy or our sacrifice. It was not simply a matter of sex —at least where Nellie was concerned. Perhaps it was a mingling of pride and self pity. Crippled herself, she mistook me for a complete person. Nellie in her wheel-chair will never know that I am more crippled than her . . .'

'What do you mean by that?' asked Elsa.

I told her how my decline set in the day I parted from Nellie. How, from that day until now I had lived like a hunted animal. I spoke to her about Heather and the torture I had been through. She knew something about my feelings for Heather, but had no clear idea about the nature of our relationship. I spelled out, without dwelling on the sexual side of our relationship, how I had been cheated and be- trayed and how miserable I was.

'It is my one wish to see you happy,' she said with emotion.

I was touched by her kindness. I put my hand on her knees and said, 'Marry me then.'

Thus it was finalised. Meditating on a dead man and a crippled girl, I was consigned to life with a woman I did not love.

Elsa took the arrangement of our marriage entirely into

her hands. She informed her mother and got her consent; she placed an announcement of our engagement in the local paper, though few knew us; she ordered a wedding cake and paid for it; she arranged for a quiet Anglican ceremony in her mistress's basement; she bought herself a wedding-gown, and a brown Burton suit for me.

Her master and mistress, and their children, were the only people who attended our wedding. The ceremony was brief, but painful. The minister looked vicious. I felt weak in the knees as I pondered over his words, directed chiefly at me: 'To have and to hold from this day forward, for better for worse, for richer for poorer, in sickness and in health, to love and to cherish, till death us do part.'

'With this ring I thee wed.' I slipped the wedding band on Elsa's little finger. Couldn't get it on the third finger—though she had tried it only a week ago and it fitted perfectly. Elsa had started putting on weight: today she tips the scale at 180.

Two weeks later, Heather married the Syrian—Ahmed Moustafa Sadat. They left for Damascus the next day. Heather had given up the idea of taking her degree, and Moustafa didn't need one: his father owned acres and acres of sand in Syria.

17

Heather's departure from England helped me to settle down to my studies more than my marriage to Elsa. We rented a small, dilapidated flat on Kelso Road, and at the kitchen table I wrote furiously. Elsa continued working for the Jewish doctor, not because we needed money (her mother had presented her with two thousand pounds) but because she loved children. She had planned on having four of her own: two boys and two girls. I froze at the thought of children: four summer sausages, for that's what they would look like. And all from a woman I didn't love, a woman with the quaint notion that she could make me happy.

The days were bearable, for my studies kept me occupied. But the evenings and nights were full of torment. I couldn't make love to her unless I closed my eyes and imagined I was with Heather. And her big body sprawled next to mine made me loathe her. And her enthusiasm for good living and food sickened me. Though we had taken the flat for only three months, Elsa set about wall-papering it. And she bought scores of potted plants and watered them till I felt like sending for the chaplain. She had a passion for shopping and scanned the local paper for 'the sales' in the city. She would go five miles to buy tins of peas and potatoes because they were a penny cheaper. It wasn't that she was stingy, but she prided herself in being a thrifty housewife. Once she came back with six dozen frankfurters.

'What are we going to do with all this?' I asked. 'I hate frankfurters, and we don't have a fridge to store them.'

'They were very cheap—only four-and-six a dozen!'

'Cheap indeed! But what are we going to do with them? They will start rotting in three days.'

That hadn't occurred to Elsa, and for a moment she looked perplexed. But for a moment only—Elsa can always think up something.

'I'll finish them in three days,' she said, triumphantly. And her face glowed at having found so easy a remedy.

And, by God, she did! She earned an upset stomach though, but she remained cheerful. For three days I slept on the floor, and I slept bloody soundly. That was the way to keep away from the bed, I figured. Give her frankfurters and let her fart. A blanket on the floor and a bottle of cologne was all I needed to preserve my sanity. However, Elsa had much faith in the marriage bed, and I climbed back in again.

Why did I marry Elsa? There are a thousand and one reasons—and for all seasons. I wanted to get away from Heather; I wanted to live a clean and virtuous life; I believed in the Scriptures; I was tired; I wanted a home; I didn't know what I was doing; I was lonesome; Elsa loved me; I was caught by Elsa in an unguarded moment; I lacked the guts to say no; I was deceived; and I loved Elsa. I have turned them over in my mind a thousand times.

One mustn't ask questions, one should seek antidotes. I couldn't divorce Elsa so soon after marriage. And I had no grounds for divorce. I could run away from her. But where to? She could find another man? Not likely. She could die a natural death? Very unnatural. She neither smoked nor drank, and I hadn't heard of anybody dying of frankfurters. I could kill myself? No. I might as well live with Elsa. She wasn't a bad woman, and she had a good heart. I wish it was weak. Elsa dying of heart failure was at best a remote possibility. None the less I asked her if she preferred cremation to burial.

I got my degree in June. Elsa took the day off to attend the convocation and was greatly impressed by the ceremony. She thought it was a great honour that I had the opportunity to kneel before the Chancellor—the Queen's cousin—and that I had conducted myself handsomely. I walked four steps backwards, instead of the two, before making my exit. If I had taken one more step, I would have fallen off the dais. I wish I had: Elsa would have had less to clap about.

My professor called me to his home for tea. He was happy with my thesis and said it wasn't bad. Like my uncle, he exhorted me to return to India and do something for my country. But I didn't want to go back. I was afraid of Elsa haggling over prices in the vegetable market.

'Have you considered Canada?' asked Dr Adams. 'It is a fairly civilised place. You will find all the amenities of life there, if you believe in them. I sent two of my students there; never heard from them, though I am sure they did very well for themselves. It is snowbound most of the year, but the climate is healthy. You don't catch anything more than a common cold.'

And so it was Canada. I felt I could really make a fresh start in a new country. My professor sent off a letter and within weeks I was offered a teaching position in Erigon College of Liberal Arts.

On July 29th—my birthday—Elsa and I left for Erigon by Air Canada. Elsa wanted a seat next to the window, and so we went to Heathrow Airport two hours before departure time. The trip was pleasant enough, though I felt the plane tipped a little to the left—the side on which we two sat. but I don't think we were in any serious danger.

18

Soon after we arrived the Chairman of the History Department, Professor Patrick Dunlop, invited us for drinks. Dunlop had taken his Ph.D. from a university in the British Midlands, and like me had been advised to try his fortunes in Canada. Before coming to Erigon eight years ago, he had been on a skiing holiday in the Swiss Alps and within weeks had fallen in love and married a Swiss girl called Petra. They had four boys—all with running noses.

Dunlop was a small man with moist lips and a fine, pointed beard. You couldn't imagine him without his beard —he must have been born with it. But the most arresting thing about him was his eyes: sad, grimy and frightened like the eyes of Salamano's dog. He spoke quickly and nervously. 'To put in quotation marks' was his favourite phrase, and every time he used it he would raise both his hands and wiggle his index fingers. This was not surprising, for he had edited two volumes of the sayings of great men for a publisher in Minot, North Dakota. He was by far the most published man in our Department. His wife was tall and skinny, and very convincing in all she said. She spoke German fluently and became a good friend of Elsa's—and managed to sell us their house.

We were twelve teachers in the History Department: eight men and four women. The women were wives of history professors of established reputation, who had served the college with distinction, took active part in committee work, and spoke every second January at the Prairie Historical Conference. I was told that the History Department was a large, happy family. But it had not always been so. There was a fellow called Cursetjee—a newspaper man from Calcutta who had earned his Ph.D. from Trinity College, Dublin, for a thesis on the Irish Potato Famine of 1845. He had created much enmity by publicly stating that the Canadians have no history to talk about. He left in a huff for Berkeley two years ago, and since then there had been peace. I heard more about Cursetjee that evening—perhaps because he was an Indian like me—than about anybody else. He was described to me variously as a gentleman, a scholar, an editor, a go-getter, a hack writer, a plagiarist, and a bounder. What led to his departure was the initiation of the *Notikeewin Historical Review*, of which he wanted to be the editor. And there were many who thought that he should be the editor. But he didn't have a wife to promote his case, and the choice fell on Dr Horace Peabody: a dapper little man with a handlebar moustache, who walked with an awkward, shuffling gait. He had never edited a magazine, but his wife owned an art shop and was the President of the Faculty Wives' Association—a most powerful body on campus. He also had the most colourful doctoral gown west of Suez, which he wore when engaged in solemn pursuits such as editing and writing poetry.

Dr Peabody was among the first persons to befriend me, once I had satisfied him that I didn't know Cursetjee and had full confidence in his own editorship. Talking to him, I gathered that the *Notikeewin Historical Review* had been started as a serious research journal, but owing to the lack of suitable articles it had begun publishing stories and poems on historical themes. Peabody had been married several times, and some of his friends thought he had in him the makings of a major poet. He had written some fifty poems: all on the themes of marriage and divorce. His 'divorce poems' had been published in one magazine or the other, but he had failed to get even a single of his 'marriage poems' accepted. This irked Mrs Peabody, and she herself applied to the Research Committee for a grant of $500 to finance the publication of her husband's tributes to her. There was, of course, no question of the sum being refused. Mrs Peabody had already designed the dust-jacket: it showed two wedding-bells dangling like testicles.

The party began well, but finished badly for us. Nobody talked shop as they do in England: one's learning is looked upon as more personal than one's wife. After a few drinks the men were as fed horses in the morning: each neighing after his neighbour's wife. Two horses trotted up to Elsa and whinnied. Elsa giggled and laughed and blushed, but she kept sitting so that no one got a chance to stroke her arse. I was proud to see my wife so desired by other men. By midnight all the guests had left, and I stood alone with Elsa and my hosts.

Professor Dunlop asked me if I had thought of buying a house. Before I could open my mouth, his wife observed that a house in the flourishing city of Erigon was the best possible investment. Renting was throwing money down the drain. Elsa nodded, and asked how best to go about buying a house.

'You can have ours,' said Professor Dunlop. 'It is an old house, and old houses are hard to come by.'

'I wouldn't stay a day in one of those modern homes,' added Petra Dunlop. 'They are so uncomfortable, and they don't have a fireplace.'

Elsa agreed that old houses were more comfortable to live in. And immediately we were taken on a tour of the house. I hated the idea of buying a house, especially an old one with crooked rooms and corners.

'Is there a garage?' I asked.

'A garage? You don't have garages in old homes! These were built before the ugly monsters came in,' said Mrs Dunlop admonishingly. 'And what do you want a garage for? We park ours on the street. You drive straight off without backing up.'

My inquiry about the garage led Professor Dunlop to ask me if I would care to buy his Armstrong Siddeley. Like his house, the car was old. But nothing ever went wrong with Armstrong Siddeleys, except that the firm which manufactured them went bankrupt. By the time we left, it appeared that we might have to buy the Professor's car as well as his house.

Elsa bought the house. Mrs Dunlop phoned her day and

night to persuade her to buy it, and with every phone call she would reduce the down payment. Elsa wouldn't come out and say 'no', but kept asking me what she should do.

'Tell Petra to go and get herself screwed,' I said.

Elsa objected violently to my language, and I think it was to spite me that she bought the house. Anyway, she made the down payment from the money her mother had given her. I think it was $2,000. And a monthly payment of $155 for perhaps as long as we lived. Then the house would be ours and we would have to pay the municipal rates and taxes only. And these were not high in this district.

Peabody, my dearest friend in the Department, swore I had been badly cheated. But he saw some good in the trans-action: Dunlop couldn't refuse me tenure after selling his house to me. Peabody was right. And he helped me to wriggle out of buying the Prof's car. I was to tell Dunlop I wanted an automatic. As Professor Dunlop himself was thinking of acquiring an automatic, he did not press me too far. However, he reduced the price from $250 to $150. But Peabody had asked me not to pay a cent more than $50, and he later sold me his own 1956 Ford for $100. It gave me trouble-free service for five weeks, after which I traded it for $25.

Before the term began, we had moved into the Pro-fessor's house on Edgar Street, overlooking the Imperial Oil Refinery and Sampax Iron Works. The Professor had rented a new split-level home in Whitewood Park, as old houses were hard to come by. Elsa settled down to re-papering the walls, scraping and polishing the woodwork, contacting electricians and plumbers to deal with the odd things that need attention in a house so hard to come by! I began preparing my lectures. I had three different courses to teach: Freshman History 135.11 (an introduction to the significant aspects of the methods of history); European History 274.95 (a study of civilisation in the West from the 5th to the 15th centuries); and British History 285.27 (political and baronial conflict under the Lancastrians and the Yorkists).

19

I had thought that to be lonesome was to be alone. I discovered that to be lonesome was to be with people one did not love. And I liked no one around me. The big, happy family—the History Department—was a fiction. It was torn with envy and strife. Everyone hated someone, and I hated them all. Murder, betrayal, perfidy, treachery, rebellion, massacre, cruelty, rage, madness, lust, malice, rape, plunder, extortion, these were the lessons of history. And I prepared my lectures diligently. But the students were not interested. Some yawned, some slept, some winked, a few took down notes, and the rest stayed away from classes. There were those who asked me questions, and they were always the same: How many marks for the term paper? How long should the essay be? Do you want footnotes? How many questions in the exam? Should we write on both sides of the answer-book? Do you deduct marks for spelling? Do you fail students?

I failed no one. They were all damned souls: as damned as my shifty colleagues angling for positions and promotions. As damned as Heather with Moustafa and I with Elsa. As damned as the whole human race. And it was from this understanding of damnation that an all-embracing, Christ-like compassion took possession of me. I was as old as Christ, I had suffered like Christ, and I must be crucified like Christ. I ordered a life-size cross for myself and stood it against the wall of my basement study. Under it I would stand for hours with my arms stretched and my head slouched, while Elsa was out shopping or gossiping. I donned a beard; I ordered a red robe.

The enrolment in my class swelled when it got known that

I didn't fail students, but the attendance fell. The students loved me, and I loved them all. When girls came up to me, I smiled and told them, 'Woman, what have I to do with thee?' Still they persisted, and wanted to know why I had given them a C+ or a B—. I told them that I was not infallible, but that He is, and if it were a matter of their salvation I would intercede with the Heavenly Father on their behalf. What do earthly grades matter?

A few students complained about me to Professor Dunlop. He laughed and sent them away. He told me that the Canadians, though a kindly people, were prosaic, and that they couldn't appreciate my subtle sense of humour which I surely must have acquired in England.

I had given up sex altogether: every thought of it. But I still had erections in the mornings and it bothered me. I went to my good physician, Doctor Ledebur, and begged him to castrate me. He flatly refused, and this cost me my sainthood.

Elsa became pregnant.

I nailed the cross to the ceiling of my study, I tore my robe into shreds, I shaved off my beard. I was not only a sinner, but a begetter of sins. Myself lost, I was bringing into the world my facsimile who must re-enact the human drama, suffer like me, and through copulation pass on affliction and wretchedness to others. With my death, only I would die; the evil in me would live on.

Knowing Elsa, I did not suggest an abortion. Instead, I went to see her doctor.

'Any hope of the child dying during birth?' I asked.

'What?' queried the doctor, incredulously.

'The child! Any risks to his life?'

'Ah, I understand you now,' he said, leaning back on his swivel chair. 'Don't worry at all. Your wife is a very healthy person and I foresee no complications.'

'None?'

'No. But ask her to see me every fortnight. Do you want a boy or a girl?'

'Something in between, doctor.' I meant a eunuch, something that couldn't copulate.

'You mean twins?'

I nearly fainted. It had never occurred to me that I could be the father of twins. As soon as I got home I lay down on the floor of my study, looking steadily at the cross. With hands joined in supplication, I prayed loudly enough to bring down Elsa from the kitchen, 'Jesus Christ, my Lord, my Father, I will take anything but twins. Have mercy on me.'

Elsa gave birth to a ten-pound boy. With surprising ease. Forty minutes after the labour pangs, and ten minutes after she was admitted into the maternity ward, the ugliest conceivable mass of contorted flesh gave a terrific howl, announcing to the world that I was a father. The faculty wives had a heyday tracing the boy's features to me, though he looked like the very devil himself. This was the meanest cut of all, but these women were a vicious lot. The day after Elsa got home they had a shower for the baby. Feeding bottles, blankets, frocks, diapers, piss pots, toys and a clutter of baby-goods were dropped at our door-step. I had to write little 'Thank You' notes for all this garbage.

I had to offer my Department colleagues the customary cigars. I bought a box of twenty of the cheapest brand and left it on the secretary's table. Within minutes the box was empty, though only six people smoked. The Chairman alone (though a professed non-smoker) took five cigars; Peabody took four (I don't grudge him anything), and the secretary took one. I don't know where the rest went. Two members of the Department—husband and wife—got none, and I had to buy them cigars of their choice from the college bookshop.

Every cloud has its silver lining. And this cloud on the cot wasn't without one. I discerned that I could now leave Elsa without any qualms, for the boy would provide her solace and wipe the tears—if any—that she might shed at my departure. She was, I could see, so wrapped up in the baby that she would forget even to sew on my buttons. She would not miss me! And this thought was comforting.

After the birth of the boy, I had lost faith in Christ. Not completely, for He could have easily given me twins. I had also read Hermann Hesse's *Siddhartha* and had been captivated by the saga of Gautama. The need to renounce the world and to preach the doctrine of non-violence was expedited by the brutalities of the Americans in Vietnam. I wanted to go to Indo-China and walk the Ho-Chi-Minh Trail, imparting to all the 'noble eight-fold path'. I was near making this momentous decision and shaving my head, when I was struck blind in the left eye.

20

Guess who came today? Marie! My lovely, charming girl. Exactly six weeks to the day she delivered the groceries. And she didn't bring anything for me, but herself. She came to find out how I was keeping. I was typing, when the doorbell rang. I peeped through the curtains. There she stood, bewitching.

We ran into a little misunderstanding, but it was soon cleared up. I thought she had been sent by Elsa to spy on me. So I didn't ask her in immediately, but fetched the Bible and made her repeat the following words after me, 'I swear I do not know any woman in Erigon who weighs 180 pounds and has the most hideous-looking boy.'

Though she giggled while she swore, I believe her. She is so innocent and pure.

She wandered through the house, leisurely, confidently. She evinced none of the fears I had seen in her the first time she came. She asked me why I kept the curtains drawn, why I slept in the living-room instead of the bedroom, what I was writing. I evaded her questions. But I am going to sleep in the bedroom tonight. Marie is right. Why not sleep in a bed when you can afford one? I didn't tell her I was afraid someone might get in beside me. Marie, if it would only be you, I would never leave the bed. Do you know, my little girl, that if I were to bury the right side of my face into the pillow—the world would go utterly dark. When I am dead and gone, Marie, would you have the courage to tell the world that you walked through these rooms one September morning with a one-eyed man?

After Marie had toured the house, we did some target practice from the bedroom window. I put a few more holes in the CANCER-CAN-BE-BEATEN can. Marie quickly learnt to handle a gun, but I couldn't teach her how to aim. I was a bit concerned about wasting my precious cartridges. I asked her if there was an undertaker in Corwind.

'No,' she laughed. 'We'll send one for you from Erigon.'

I was very worried. It had never occurred to me that there wouldn't be an undertaker in this town.

'You promise me you will send for one,' I pleaded.

'If I am still here,' she chuckled.

'What do you mean?'

'Well, I have a job in Vancouver. I start work in November.'

'You are not going away, Marie! And why did you go to Vancouver without telling me? Do you know what happened while you were away? I went to the shop to see you, and I mistook your sister for you.'

'Dad and sis told me about it. They think you are very funny. All writers are funny people, aren't they?'

'Don't go in November. Go in December. I am also going in December.'

'Where do you go?'

I didn't tell her. I wasn't going back to Elsa or to my job. I looked at my gun. I couldn't tell Marie I had but a short time on earth, and that I wanted to spend it with her. A heaviness came over me, and she sensed my despair.

'Why have you gone sad?' she asked. 'You were so cheerful a few minutes ago.'

'I am lonely, Marie.'

'You miss Nellie, I suppose.'

I said nothing. Better that the shadows of Nellie should hang between us. Better that she knew nothing of Heather and Elsa and my blind eye. She would not understand, and now there was no time. In November she goes. December I go. And this is September. Thirty Septembers had already gone.

'Come, Marie,' I said stretching out my hands. 'Let's go for a walk.'

She took my hand in hers and we sauntered towards the River Quimperle. In silence. I was the first to speak.

99

'Do you know that this is my first walk out, except for the two trips I made to your shop?'

'You don't like walking?'

I did not know what to say. I felt I had harboured far too many secrets to establish any human relationship. And yet I would have told Marie about myself, if only I had known where to begin. And if the end were not so close. I pressed her hand. She smiled affectionately.

'Marie, tell me something. Why did you come to see me?'

'No, you first answer my question. Don't you like walking?'

'I do. I walked the Yorkshire dales one summer. With a girl. She knew the names of all the flowers and trees that grew there. Then winter came. . . . Now you answer my question.'

'I wanted to see you.'

'Why?'

'I guess . . . because I like you.'

'Do you think I am mad?'

'No, not at all.'

'I remember your words—I wrote them down. You said, "You are mad, completely mad. Mother told me so: you made her raise her hand and saw eight fingers on it." '

'Did you?' exclaimed Marie. 'Dad always jokes about it to mum—says she has eight fingers.'

'Some see more, and some see less. Perhaps I am mad.'

'No, you are not. You are different from others, and I love you for that.'

'Love me? You love me, Marie?'

'I like you,' she said, correcting herself.

'But I love you.'

'You don't. You hardly know me!'

She was right in her own simple way. It was difficult to explain that knowing a person had little to do with love, that all I had come to know I had learnt to hate.

We came to the river, and lay down on our backs beside each other, still holding hands. A whiff of low cloud was swiftly sailing towards the white moon. I looked at my watch to see how long it would take to cross the moon.

'What are you thinking?'

'Nothing. I am timing the passing of the cloud.'

'You time everything!'

'Yes. I am running out of time.'

'I don't understand. Have I said something I shouldn't have? Why are you so depressed?'

I turned on my side, and kissed her softly. I raised my body and brought it to rest against hers. She opened her mouth, and breathed her warm breath into my mouth. I undid the buttons of her blouse, and buried my face between her breasts. With difficulty I held back my tears; I had no reason to weep.

After a few minutes, I sat up beside her and did up the buttons of her blouse.

'There! You are fit to go home.'

'Yes, I must go now.'

'Before you go, tell me something about yourself. Do you have a boy-friend?'

She looked up at the sky and scratched her head.

'I don't mean Jesus,' I said.

Marie laughed. 'I think you are amusing.'

'Where is your boy-friend?'

'In Vancouver. He is not what you would call a boy-friend; I met him only a few times.'

'Is he nice?'

'I think so.'

'Tell me more. What does he do?'

'Joe is a carpenter.'

'Have you made love with him?'

'You shouldn't ask such questions.'

'Perhaps not. But now that I have asked?'

'Yes.'

'I love you for being so frank. Did you like it?'

'Sort of . . . it hurt my back.'

'Why?'

'It was on the floor.'

I laughed.

'Why are you laughing?'

'Surely a carpenter could have made himself a bed. Is he

on Welfare?'

Marie laughed, too. 'You're wicked. But now you tell me all about yourself.'

'I have trodden the winepress alone; and of the people there was none with me: for I will tread them in my anger, and trample them in my fury; and their blood shall be sprinkled upon my garments, and I will stain all my raiment.'

'Come, be serious. Do you have a girl-friend?'

'No.'

'You are lying.'

'I have not lied to you so far, Marie. And I don't want to lie. Therefore ask me no questions. Before long I shall tell you everything about myself, when it no longer matters. Will you come and see me tomorrow?'

'I'll phone you.'

'I don't have a phone.'

'How come?' she said, standing up and brushing the grass off her dress. I was still sitting and thinking up an excuse, when she left.

I lay down and fell asleep. When I awoke it was approaching darkness. Trudging back home I thought of Nellie, and my mother. It would be morning in Bombay. A hired hand will have given Nellie her tea in bed, and helped her to strap on her wooden legs. She will be sitting in the balcony watching the surging crowds jog and trot to work; people pushing, elbowing and jostling one another. Do not envy them, my love. They are all hurrying to their damnation. See, and understand, how far my legs have carried me. You should not have pushed me away when I came to see you. I cannot walk much longer. I am tired.

Mother, you must be getting ready to go to Willingdon. I can see you in your white stockings and your white uniform. Did you sleep soundly, Mother? And were you alone last night? I don't accuse you, Mother. I am your blood, and you are my blood. Do you remember old Belton? He loved you, and wanted to marry you. But he asked you to send me away. You slapped his face. Blood is thicker than water. But time has thinned it. I wish you had married Belton. Will you miss me, Mother?

21

I told Marie everything about myself. Everything, except Heather. Heather no longer matters to me, just as the wheels that went over Nellie's legs do not matter to her. These things are like Providence, one does not accuse them.

Marie comes to me every day. She goes straight to the bath to wash her feet. Then she comes and stands before me bare-footed. I remove her clothes, one by one, till she stands naked. I then lift her up and lay her on my bed—on her back.

The ritual begins. I take her feet in my two hands and press them together and kiss them. I kiss her toes several times and then I move up, inch by inch, kissing the length of her legs till I come to her sex. We don't have sex, it doesn't seem important. I continue my journey, pausing awhile on her breasts, neck, chin and lips. I rest on her lips, rubbing my nose against her nose, licking her eyes. Her eyelashes glisten with my saliva. It takes about fifteen minutes; I don't keep my watch on the bed to time it.

Today, after the ritual, while I lay beside her, I saw from the window the first snow of the year coming down in tiny flakes. I thought of December. I asked her if I could make love to her.

'Yes,' she whispered, holding my face between her hands and looking into my eyes.

I withdrew. I went and sat in a chair and covered myself with a sheet.

'What's the matter?' she asked, timidly.

'You should know something about me, before we go any further. I should have told you earlier, but I couldn't. It was not simply that I was frightened of losing you. Perhaps

I was frightened of losing you, having begun to love you. But all this is beside the point. After you have heard me you will walk out of that door. So you might as well get into your clothes.'

She lay transfixed, unconscious of her alluring body. At last she spoke, 'What is it, Tristan?'

'I am married. I have a wife and son in Erigon. I have left them both, and I am hiding here. I have only a few weeks of life left. You've seen the gun—You now know all . . . no, not yet.'

'Go on. Don't hide anything from me.'

'I am blind. I can't see. That is I can't see with my left eye. Your father and mother laughed, but it wasn't funny.'

'I am sorry,' she said with hushed breath. 'Come, come near me.'

I obeyed. I sat beside her.

'Lie down with me.'

'No.'

'Please.'

I lay down. I covered my face with my hands.

'Tristan, my darling, come. Take me.'

'Marie! A married man? A blind man? What will you answer your God?'

'He may not question me.'

'He may.'

'Then I shall tell Him I loved you with all the love He had made me capable of. Here, let me hold you.'

I felt the warmth of her body permeate my own, till we melted and dissolved into each other. When we regained our separate identities and were two people again, she stood up to dress. I did not help her with her clothes as I had always done. I lay on the bed watching her.

She came over and kissed me. I held her face between my hands, as she had held mine an hour ago. I kissed her on the forehead.

'Take care,' she said.

'And you too. Goodbye, my love.'

She did not answer, but smiled sadly and left.

For the first time in my life I am composed, serene. She

has gone forever from my life, leaving just two words with me, 'Take care.' I shall, dearest of all. Tonight.

Goodbye Marie, goodbye Nellie, and you too Elsa. Goodbye dear Mother. Flesh of your flesh? No more. Dust unto dust.

22

I didn't kill myself last night. I am damn glad I didn't, for Marie came to see me this morning. She was very angry at what I was going to do and said that if I killed myself she would never speak to me again. And that is one thought I can't bear.

Don't think I am a coward because I didn't kill myself. I am not afraid of death, but I couldn't push the barrel down my throat for two reasons. First, I remembered how it had set me coughing the time John came to deliver the groceries. Second, the bullet might just go down and lodge in my stomach. And there are no doctors in Corwind I would trust my life to. The only assured way to die would be to blow out my brains. But the barrel is so long that after I had pressed it to my temple I couldn't get my finger on the trigger. So I decided to saw off two feet of the barrel.

I had sawn off the barrel and was drilling a hole to put in the bead, when Marie came. She said it was cowardly to kill oneself, and any fool could do it. If that were true, I remarked, would she explain why the world was so full of people?

'Because the average man is sane,' she said.

'Are you implying that I am mad?'

'No, but you have problems.'

'You mean Elsa?'

She asked me about my life with Elsa. I told her everything about myself, beginning with Heather. I spared no details, for once I began speaking I felt the need to unburden myself. Marie listened intently, and interrupted me only once to ask if there actually were birth control pills which men could take instead of women. She smiled occasionally, but she was not laughing at me. There were tears in her eyes when I narrated how I spent the night ringing the door-bell while Heather was making love to Moustafa Sadat.

Surprisingly, I had not much to say about Elsa, though we had been married for three years. I told her the circumstances which led to our marriage, Elsa's interest in flowers, in buying a house, in being a mother, a thrifty housewife, etc. I should perhaps have mentioned that she was the only woman who took any interest in my studies. But what good would that have done?

After I had finished, Marie remarked, 'I don't see anything wrong with Elsa. I think she is worth her weight in gold.'

'Indeed! Do you know how much she weighs?'

'No.'

'A hundred and eighty pounds.'

'What has that to do with your dislike of her?'

I had never asked myself that question, and had no answer. But then one does not live one's life by questions and answers. One accepts the world with one's senses. Would Marie explain why some people like garlic and others don't? Elsa could have been a world and a half to someone else, to me she was just a fright. And I told Marie so.

Marie did not understand. She felt my past experiences with people made me react the way I did. And she was shocked at my attitude towards my son.

'Perhaps you were not meant for Elsa and your marriage to her was a mistake. But how can you hate your own son?'

'I don't hate him.'

'But you don't love him?'

'No.'

'I have never heard of a father who did not love his own child.'

'Love is not going to help him, Marie. When I look at him I see into his future, and the torture that awaits him. I brought him into this world to suffer. It was a pure accident —but he will suffer all the same. Suffering is the only legacy he will inherit from me.'

'You are sick, and you see everything only from the angle

107

of your own unhappy self.'

'If I am sick, wouldn't it be better that I kill myself? No one is going to miss me.'

'I am,' she said sharply. 'And I am not going to let you do anything so foolish.'

She clasped me in her arms and held me close. I felt a new stirring in me, and the desire to live. But it was short-lived. She asked me if I was really blind. I moved away from her quickly as one would from a leper. I wanted none of her charity nor her love.

'Yes, I am blind. Stone blind in the left eye.'

'What happened?'

'Does it matter what happened? The retina got detached.'

'No. I don't think it matters.'

'Not to you. You have your two eyes. Neither to me, for I won't need the other one.'

'What have I said?' she asked, bewildered. 'Why do you talk like that?'

'It was good of you to have come. But our paths are very different. You go your way and let me go mine.'

'Don't say such things. You are very dear to me; how am I to convince you?'

'Marie, you too are very, very dear to me. But you have come into my life much too late. You cannot help me, but you can do yourself a lot of harm. I am a husband of a woman I do not love, I am a father of a child I do not want, and I am blind as well. It is none of your fault that this should have happened to me. Please, do not pity me. Leave me to face the reality of my life.'

'But that is exactly what I want you to do. To face life, not to give up. And I want to be with you to help you.'

'How can you help me?'

She had not thought of that. She looked at me as if she were begging pardon for having said something foolish.

'Marie, I understand you. You must try to understand me. You were right when you said I was mad.'

'I never called you mad.'

'Even if you did, what difference would it make. All this argument is taking us nowhere. Come, kiss me goodbye.

Think of me and pray for me. When you are married, and have a home and children of your own—call one of them Tristan.'

'Stop it,' she cried. 'Why must you torture me?'

I put my arm round Marie and led her to the bedroom. I stood for a while staring vacantly at the bed. I was tired and wanted to rest, but not with Marie beside me in the bed. So I led her back into the living-room, and lay down on the carpet and fell asleep. When I awoke, I found my head in Marie's lap, and her smoothing out my hair with her long fingers. I felt tranquil. We kept looking into each other's faces, till she smiled.

'Say something nice to me,' she coaxed.

'If I had another life, Marie, I would spend every minute of it loving you, holding you, worshipping you—'

'Why not this life, Tristan?'

'It is already spent.'

'It isn't. You have just begun life ... you can make a fresh start.'

'I did. Twice! The first time with Heather, and then with Elsa. Where are they both now? One gone mad, the other deserted. And I on the brink of death.'

'You are not on the brink of death. You have still so much to give to the world.'

'I have nothing to give to the world.'

'All right. But you can give much to me. For my sake—promise me you will do yourself no harm.'

'What would you like me to do, Marie?'

'I have thought it all out while you were sleeping. You don't have to go back to Elsa if you don't want to. You just stay with me. As soon as I start working and have found a room, you come and live with me. Will you?'

'What will I do in Vancouver?'

'Anything you like. You don't have to do anything. I will work and look after you and give you all you want. In the day while I am gone, you can write. When I come back in the evenings—you love me.'

'I can cook for you. I am good at frying mushrooms.'

'I love mushrooms.'

'So did Heather.'

'You mustn't think of Heather any more—not of anyone. Do you understand?'

'Yes, Marie. What you say is so beautiful. But suppose I go blind while you are away.'

'You will never go blind, my Tristan, I assure you. Your fear is your excuse to run away from all the things you do not like. If you didn't have this excuse, you would find another.'

Marie may be right, you know. I was thinking of renouncing the world and walking the Ho-Chi-Minh Trail, preaching the doctrine of non-violence before I lost my eye. Where would I have been now? The Americans would have bombed me out. It's good I lost my eye, so that I can be with Marie. It is better to be here. It is better not to think.

23

I think a lot. At times I am full of hope and very elated, at others everything seems illusory and I am frightfully depressed. I am in a quandary: I keep thinking all the time. Marie tells me not to think, she keeps saying everything will work out well. But for how long? How long can I stay with Marie? How can I marry her unless I am divorced from Elsa? And on what grounds could I get a divorce? And who is going to support her and the boy? And what about my job in Erigon?

I fear Marie doesn't know what she is doing. She can't live her whole life as my mistress. And what about her family? What will the parents say when they find out that their daughter is living with a married man? I have been persuading Marie to tell them the truth about me, but she won't. She says she will tell them when the time comes. So far, all that her family knows about me is that I am a professor who has taken six months off from teaching to write a book. Marie says she will tell them one of these days that I am a divorcee.

Her parents have been pressing me to spend an evening with them. I have been putting off the invitation, for I suspect they will ask me questions, and I can't lie. I mean, I don't want to lie. Marie occasionally brings her sister Marion to visit me, and I feel uncomfortable. I fear she might ask me awkward questions. But she doesn't. She is a sweet girl and very much like my Marie. I like her because she acts and talks so much like my Marie. If I were to wed Marie by proxy, Marion would be the girl.

Marie says I think too much and get myself tied up in knots, that I should learn to take things one at a time. She finds there is nothing wrong in my coming and living with her—that later on I could obtain a divorce and marry her. After all, many people do that. Why should I be frightened? One has only one life to live and one should live it as one feels best. If people talk, what difference would that make? Would I rather people didn't talk and I was unhappy, or that people talked and I was happy? I am not afraid of gossips, having lived three years in Erigon, but I don't know where I am heading to. Marie is right: it takes more courage to live than to die. But I am no hero, and I would rather take the easier way out. I cannot help feeling that the easier way out is the best way out for all concerned. I would be out of pain. Elsa might mourn my death for a while, and lose some weight, but it will do her no harm. Besides, she will be able to collect my insurance. Marie will find someone else. She is so young and beautiful. I tell Marie that mine is the best solution to the problem. But Marie is like Elsa in one respect: once she has made up her mind you can't dislodge her. She doesn't even allow me to mention the word 'die'. So I have to set about dying subtly.

I asked Marie what her reactions would be if I were to go back to Elsa. She said she would not object, for Elsa was my wife.

'If you can let me go to Elsa, why not let me go my own way?'

'No,' she said firmly. 'You either stay with me or go to Elsa. But I won't have you doing anything mad.'

'I can't go back to Elsa. At times I really wish I could, it would make things so much easier for you. And it would ease my conscience.'

'Is your conscience troubling you?'

'It does, occasionally. I feel I have been very unjust to Elsa. I never felt so till you made me speak about her the other day. I married her thinking only of myself, and when I found that she was not what I wanted—I discarded her like an old garment. It is not her fault that I do not love her as I love you.'

'Nor is it yours, Tristan. You married her with the best of intentions.'

112

'I have begun to doubt that. When I married her I was thinking only of my happiness—some way to save myself. I now find comfort in the thought that if I have brought unhappiness to her, I have not spared myself. For me to begin my life again, thinking only of myself, would be vile.'

'But you are not thinking only of yourself. As long as you are unhappy you cannot give happiness to others. And then there is me, too.'

'Have you ever considered the possibility, Marie, that one day I may have no use for you?'

'If I were to consider every possibility, Tristan, I would be afraid to live. One must leave something to God.'

'Only if one has lived a virtuous life. What can a sinner leave to God but his punishment?'

'Oh, so now you think you are a sinner! From Jesus Christ to Buddha to a sinner. What will you be next, my dear Tristan? A murderer!'

'Don't laugh at me, Marie.'

'I am not laughing at you. But I want you to understand once and for all that the choice before you is not between life and death, but between the things life has to offer. That means Elsa and me. And as you say, you cannot go back to Elsa. You will have to come and live with me. Do you get that?'

'It would have been easier if I had met you ten years ago.'

'But you didn't, my love.'

'I am ten years older than you are.'

'Does age make all that difference?'

'One's experiences do. A fresh start in life is a delusion. Life is not jumping off one train and climbing on to another. It is like a train to which wagons are hooked with each passing year, and you pull them along wherever you go. Do you see what I mean? My future can never be wholly freed from my past.'

'That's a lot of nonsense—and coming from a historian. If people thought the way you do, there would be no progress. We have moved from the age of horse transportation to that of cars. Does the car pull the horse behind it?'

'Marie, you are not a philosopher, but you are the loveliest person I have known. I shall do as you say, not because I have much faith in myself but because you are my last hope. And loving you means everything to me.'

'Does it, Tristan?'

'Everything.'

'Then promise me you will stop worrying and do as I tell you.'

I promised, and I felt very happy. I am very happy now at the thought of being with Marie for the rest of my life. At last my God has taken mercy on me. But I have come to my present happiness through much suffering. So do not envy me.

24

Marie is so cocksure about everything. I don't mind leaving questions of life and death in her hands, but when she contradicts me on matters concerning history and university life, I feel most offended. And I have told her so. But she loves me and has a way of laughing that prevents me from walking out on her. I don't mind criticism: as a writer I need a merciless critic, but I don't want her to question every word I say. Today I was telling Marie the important role wives can play in their husbands' academic careers.

'How can a wife help her husband?' she asked.

'In many ways, Marie. For one, she can let her bottom be pinched by his immediate superior, and that is worth one special salary increase in most cases. A pretty girl like you could get me a full professorship in two years, but I would rather suffer the indignities of an assistant professor than see an old lecher lay his paws on you.'

'Do such things really happen?'

'Yes. A wife can blackmail her husband's boss and force him to promote her husband. She can run away with another man and leave her husband to give all his energies to his work, and that too could help.'

Marie laughed. 'I don't believe you.'

'Well, how do you think I was promoted?'

'I don't know.'

'Through Elsa. She and Petra—my Chairman's wife— became the best of pals after we bought their house. And Elsa recommended me to Petra. After that it was rubber-stamped all the way up.'

'Surely important institutions aren't run like that?'

'The whole world is run like that. Living in this little

town, you have no knowledge of the ways of the world and the power that women wield. Have you ever heard of the Faculty Wives' Association?'

'No.'

'There! It is a union of wives of the teaching staff. Their weapon is slander, and they generally attack the husbands of the prettiest girls. Since Elsa wasn't pretty, I was in their good books. But God help the man they detest—and I have never seen God intervene when the fury of these wives was roused. Of course, they occasionally speak well of a man, and then he is made. I had a friend who was writing a novel he called *The Long Phuff-Phuff*. It was about a boy and a girl who met on the trans-continental train and were searching for a nook where they could make love. They had boarded the train in Montreal and were on their way to Vancouver, and their passions rose and fell with the changing speed of the train. Rather a novel idea, and very original. Now this professor was so obsessed with the theme that day and night he thought of nothing else but the train. In literature this is called "magnificent obsession", which Canadians lack. Anyway, this bloke was an American. Now his wife told the other wives that her husband was so absorbed in his novel that even in his sleep he kept sputtering 'chuck-chuck, phuff-phuff, chuck-chuck, phuff-phuff", and that his hands and legs moved alternately in circles like the wheels of a train. This soon became known all over the campus, and the literary editor of *The Hemisphere* wrote an article commending the writer's involvement with his subject. This professor got a salary raise of $750. And now he no longer "chuck-chucks" and "phuff-phuffs" in bed.'

'I hope you won't go "chuck-chuck" and "phuff-phuff" in bed.'

'Don't be silly, darling.'

'Did he complete his novel?'

'No. He pushed it aside and is now doing a book on creative writing. He feels the novel would be better if he first wrote a book on how to write. I tend to agree with him.'

Marie insists that my views on the faculty wives are prejudiced. This is certainly not the case, for I have always been their favourite and a few have shown me favours I would rather not speak about. She wanted to know more about academic life, how much work we professors put in, what we do when we are not lecturing, faculty-student relationship, and so on. Marie has never been in a university and so it was not easy to explain to her the intricacies of scholarly life. My task was made more difficult by what she had heard from her father (and unfortunately started to believe!), who had spent a year at my college.

'Dad says the profs only teach eight hours a week and spend the rest of their time goofing around.'

'That's a bloody lie, Marie. We teach a full nine hours.'

'Who am I to believe—you or Dad?'

'That's for you to decide. Would you rather believe your father who flunked his first year or me who has taught for three years?'

'Dad never flunked his exams.'

'Well, he talks as if he did. No good student would use the word "goof" for his professors. You have no idea how hard we people work. Take me for instance: I gave three different courses. I do admit one of the courses was in the area of my specialisation, but I didn't know a thing about the other two. History 135.11 and History 274.95 were—'

Marie interrupted me. 'Why do they number it that way —in decimals?'

'So they don't get mixed up with similar courses offered in the United States. We have to be on the guard all the time against the Americanisation of Canada. It is a matter of preserving our Canadian identity. Anyway, it was no joke teaching those two courses, I can tell you. I ran the classes as seminars: made the students write long essays which they read out to the class. I maintained a strictly neutral stance— rarely opened my mouth. This helped them to be original. When the students went off the track, I had to remind them of the forces which had shaped world history such as rape, plunder, arson, loot, malice, treachery, lust, etc. I also talked about repressive de-sublimation: the historical stage we are now at in the Western world. During my first year of teaching I fell sick several times, mostly with 'flu and laryngitis, and Elsa had to phone up Petra.'

'They shouldn't have asked you to teach what you didn't know. That's what Dad said, "The profs didn't know what they were talking about".'

'Does your Dad know what he is talking about? I don't wish to sound disrespectful of my future father-in-law, but he mustn't attack the academic community. Let me tell you we work very hard, and each of us is conscious of the responsibility he shoulders to future generations. When we couldn't check on the facts our students gave us, we corrected their English. And that is at the best of times a tricky job.'

'But you only taught nine hours a week! And you have five months off each year!'

I smiled at Marie's ignorance. She had picked up all the cant that the uneducated have against the intellectuals. I was surprised she didn't say we were wasting the tax-payers' money.

'Marie, I didn't expect such a remark from you after I told you of my friend's neurosis over his novel. A professor works harder than the Prime Minister, and for longer hours. Wherever he is, his mind is intriguing. The only time he is able to relax is when his students are reading their essays to the class. The divorce rate among professors is higher than in any other profession. And because of the professors' preoccupation with matters that are academic, adultery is looked upon as a minor aberration. And it is generally settled out of court by the wronged person seeking redress through visiting the other's wife.'

'I didn't know teachers were so promiscuous,' remarked Marie.

'We are not,' I said, hotly. 'You are misunderstanding the whole thing. What I am trying to tell you is that the average professor is so obsessed with intellectual pursuits that he has no time for questions over which your father might pull out his gun. A professor is a very busy person.'

'Well, what does he do, say, after his lectures?'

I had to explain to Marie that lecturing is the least important of our jobs, and the preparation still less. Our job is to keep the college going, except for the five months when we are in London, Paris, Rome, Zurich, Madrid for research. Then the secretaries run the college. But no sooner are we back than we start with our committees, memos, meetings, typing, xeroxing, duplicating, audio-visual techniques, and a hundred such things. I told her we had 235 committees with a total membership of over 2,000 people. The most important of all committees was the Committee Supreme, which spent seven months a year arguing over who ought to be promoted, and rejecting a steady stream of appeals from the disgruntled teachers. To be elected to this committee was an honour and a privilege, for it was sworn to secrecy, and a member could insinuate whatever he liked about whoever he wished. As the highest body of the college, it was above lobbying, and its decisions could not be influenced by anybody less than the President of the Faculty Wives' Association.

Marie had no idea of the time and work that goes into a committee. She found it hard to believe that no committee could begin work without approving the minutes of the previous meeting, and that alone could take half an hour—for some researcher was sure to find a misplaced colon or a comma. That we in our meetings strictly adhered to the parliamentary procedures of Westminster, with its 'points of order', 'proposing and seconding' of motions, 'amendments', 'amendments to the amendments', 'voting', 'deadlocks', 'recounts', etc. Sometimes it took an hour to vote an adjournment of the meeting. I told her how on one occasion the History Department had a meeting which began at 10 a.m. and went on till 6 p.m. before the members reluctantly adjourned for the day. Five members, after their dinner, recalled that the adjournment they had voted for a couple of hours before had not been seconded. So they returned to the committee room—in temperatures thirty below zero—to set the records right.

Being a simple girl, who had never entered the portals of learning, Marie could not appreciate our concern for scholarship. She did not know how we all endowed ourselves with a short-term and a long-term project. The short-term project was generally a book review, and here a time limit was imposed by the editor: the book had to be reviewed in the early years of its publication. But it was the long-term project which mattered, and to complete it within one's academic life was considered extremely unprofessional. Only one person completed his long-term project (in ten years, I think), and he immediately earned the loathing of his colleagues. Not only was his work described as shoddy, lacking in scholarly insight and detachment, but he was rightly labelled a liar: a fellow who had initially passed off a short-term project for a long-term one.

I briefly narrated to Marie how we scholars were required to project the fine image of the university to the community. 'Reach the Public' was a call better publicised than Rousseau's 'Return to Nature', and no professor could hope to profit by ignoring the tax-payer. Even Cursetjee, in spite of his sackful of publications, was told by the Dean that he had not yet made a contribution to the local community so outstanding as to merit a promotion. And though he went about boasting that he would never stoop to cater to the philistines, he began giving advice to the farmers on the cultivation of potatoes, and gratefully accepted nomination to the Provincial Horticulture Board. As a medievalist I could not be of much use to the forward-looking residents of Erigon. But I did project the university image by my vigorous enactment of the title role in Shirley's *The Cardinall*. It won me much applause—especially from the Eskimos and the Cree Indians when we took the play on a tour of the far North.

I wisely refrained from telling Marie anything about the dictum we live by: 'Publish or perish.' She would not understand how hundreds of my colleagues have perished on $20,000 a year, how Shelley's lament on the premature death of Keats—

> *The bloom whose petals, nipped before they blew,*
> *Died on the promise of the fruit,—*

would apply to nine-tenths of the professors who retired

after forty years of service. So I was happy when Marie changed the subject and asked me about my relationship with the students.

I told Marie I had always been popular with students because I failed no one, and readily endorsed their opinions on all matters with unfailing respect. Also, I supported their claim that they should have a voice in their own tragedy— college affairs—and no longer remain silent spectators. I voted in favour of their representation on each of the college's 235 committees. But what sky-rocketed my popularity was the 'Soup Deadlock', referred to variously by the Canadian press as 'The Soup Crisis', 'Pepsi Takes Over', and 'Doom of Capitalism'. The contract for the cafeteria had been given to a private enterprise which had been steadily losing money over the past six months. The Management decided to put up the price of soup by one cent: to sixteen cents from fifteen cents. The students protested on principle, and I gave them my unstinting support. We organised the sale of Pepsi Cola—at twenty cents a glass—in the hallway as a substitute for soup. During our fight with the Management we made a profit of $250—which was a welcome addition to our Agitation Fund. Eventually a compromise was worked out with the Management, though we actually came out the winner. They agreed to sell soup at the old price; the only concession we made was to allow them to reduce the quantity.

The 'Soup Deadlock', I assured Marie was of immense significance in the history of the Student Liberation Movement, and Erigon could rightly be proud of it. It was the first significant victory in Canada of Democratic Socialism against Imperialistic Enterprise. At this hour of triumph the students could have taken over the college, but they didn't know what to do with it. One of our difficulties has been that the average student so far spends only three years of his life in college. But once they take over the college, as they should do, they could stay on till they reached retirement or qualified for Welfare.

Marie thinks I am a born revolutionary and that I should

be wielding the sword instead of the pen. This induced me to tell her of my days as a Gentleman Cadet at the National Defence Academy in Dehra Dun. I told her I would write it out and read it to her. She said that would be good—it could make my first publication.

25

I read out to Marie the account of my career as an Army officer, which began when I was a little under twenty:

I had not thought of the Army as a career till almost the time I was selected. Mother and I got on well together, and in Delhi I enjoyed all the luxuries that go with a comfortable middle-class income. The elders of my community—many of them my self-appointed guardians—thought I should join the Police. The Police was still the one profession where Anglo-Indians were welcome for, devoid of any loyalties, they could be trusted to take no sides in the frequent Hindu-Muslim feuds. And their corruption and brutality made them feared and respected by most people. To belong to the Police force meant money and prestige, and I sought both.

But it was Colonel Melvin Ross who wheedled me into joining the Army. He had been commissioned in the last days of the British Raj, and was posted at Army Headquarters in New Delhi. His wife had eloped with a French diplomat and he, like Mother, did not know what to do with his evenings. He came regularly to our home with a bottle of whisky and occasionally asked me to join Mother and him for a drink. He was a kind, shy man, and referred to me as 'my boy'. He told me that the Indian Army was no longer what it used to be, but it was still the best service in India and the most British of all. He talked of smart salutes, care of arms, leaves, pay arrears, mess, uniforms, and ceremonies. Rituals and ceremonies had always impressed me, and I appeared before the Army Selection Board and passed. Two weeks after my batch had reported for training at Dehra Dun, I joined them.

I remember vividly my first day at the Academy. It was a Sunday, and therefore a day of rest. Huge bearded Sikhs had washed their hair and were drying it on the verandahs. They looked fierce—like maenads—and I did not want them as comrades-in-arms. I would rather fight my country's enemies alone. The sight of the barbed-wire fences, the neat gravelled walks, the howitzers and cannons adorning the well-kept lawns, made me uneasy. But an officer must get used to guns, I reminded myself. And I was—whatever I might be a month later—a Gentleman Cadet. I decided to live up to it.

I was in civvies of course, but my stride and carriage had improved perceptibly in the four hours I had been there. I thought of giving the place a good look round. I stalked out of my room bravely, after having saluted myself several times before a mirror.

'Come here,' called out someone. I turned round to see who was in trouble.

'You there! Run up,' he said to me. He was, as I learnt later, like everybody else under training, a Gentleman Cadet.

'You mean me?' I asked, sceptically.

'No, your granny,' he barked. 'Are you coming or do you want me to come and fetch you?'

I ran up and stood before him. I saluted smartly.

'You are not supposed to salute in that bloody rigout of yours. What's your name?'

'Tristan Elliott, sir.'

'Tristan Ediot! That's what you are! Aye, what's my name?'

'I don't know, sir.'

'You don't! And you know your own fuckin' name. Conceited bastard. I will teach you who I am. Now run round the block and touch all the lamp-posts and be back here in two minutes. If you are late, God help you!'

I set off at the double, and was making good time when another Gentleman Cadet on the other side of the block called out to me.

'I can't come,' I shouted. 'I have to be there in two minutes.'

'Come here,' he yelled.

I went up to him and stood to attention.

'Salute me,' he ordered.

'In civvies, sir?' I asked.

'Why? Do you want to take your pants off for me?'

'No, sir,' I said, saluting him.

'Why are you running about touching those damn posts?'

'He asked me, sir. Please let me go or else he'll get mad at me.'

'Who will get mad at you?'

'He, sir.'

'Who is he?'

'I don't know, sir.'

'You mean you are running around like a goat without even knowing whose orders you are obeying!'

'Please let me go, sir,' I begged. 'I am already late.'

'All right, skip off,' he said. 'And if he acts funny with you, tell him I stopped you.'

When I got back to the starting point, the first Gentleman Cadet was standing with his hands on his hips.

'Four minutes! You think I am your mother's lover to wait for you all day!'

'I was stopped on my way, sir,' I apologised.

'By whom?'

'I don't know, sir.'

'What? Are you telling me that you obeyed somebody's orders without even finding out his name! Learn to command. You are an officer now, not a bloody *bania* (a member of the shopkeeper class in India). Now run round the block again and be back in two minutes.'

I made it this time, and he rewarded me by telling me his name. It was Ram Gopal Agarwal (a typical *bania* name).

I returned to my room and did not venture out again for the rest of the day. I missed lunch and dinner; I had had a good breakfast at the railway station.

Next day hell broke loose. My Company Officer, a Gentleman Cadet in his final term of training, kicked at my door at 5 a.m. and got me ready for parade within minutes. He spoke in English but abused in Hindi, and there was always more Hindi than English in his orders. *Mather-chod* (rape-mother), *bahin-chod* (rape-sister), *bati-chod* (rape-daughter), *ghada-ka-lund* (penis of a donkey) were a few of the names he had time to call me the first morning, for he had to look after the welfare of thirty other cadets as well.

On the parade ground I was the only person in civvies, for all the others had reported for training the day the school commenced and had been issued shirts, shorts, uniforms, and dummy rifles. My dress—and perhaps my intellectual bearing —made me stand out in the midst of my comrades, and the Sergeant-Major rapped me a couple of times on the calves with his silver-topped baton.

The orders boomed in the air like cannons raising so much dust that I didn't know where I was. 'Left-right, left-right, left-right. Halt. Right-about-turn. Left-turn, right-turn, right-turn, left-turn, turn, turn, turn.' Soon I didn't know my left from my right, and I was afraid that if they found out they might kick me out of the Army for an idiot. However, there were two orders I could obey impeccably from the start: halt and stand-at-ease.

Another thing I could do without getting confused was mark time. But the Sergeant-Major kept yelling without a break, 'Raise your legs; higher, higher, higher'. At times I felt I might dislocate my hip joints, at others that I might knock my chin off with my knees if I went any higher. Once in a while, after I had fallen into a certain rhythm, I would close my eyes and imagine myself ascending to heaven as the cry 'higher, higher' echoed in my ears. Then suddenly I would hear 'halt' and find the Sergeant-Major's baton on my back.

My body had never ached the way it did after two hours on the parade ground. So it was a relief to get to classes to study Geography, Military History and Tactics. From 9 a.m. to 1 p.m. we moved on the double from one classroom to another. I cannot recall faithfully the things I learnt in the history class, but we were told to emulate the heroic performances of the ancient Indian kings and queens like Shivaji, Rana Partap Singh, Akbar, Ranjit Singh, Jhansi-ki-Rani and Tippoo Sultan. But what interested me most were the sand-model exercises. In a large room there was a scale model of a terrain with gaudily painted hills, rivers, train-tracks, forests, tunnels, and villages.

The instructor, a Captain, singled me out. He had a long pointer in his hand.

'Suppose,' he said, pointing to locations on the model with his pointer, 'suppose you, with an infantry battalion, were entrenched here, and your job was to defend this village. A Russian armoured division was attacking your position from the North-West, an unknown number of Chinese were poised on your Eastern flank, and the Americans were bombing you from the air. What strategy would you follow to repulse the enemy attack with the fewest casualties?'

'I would write a letter to Army Headquarters for more help,' I said.

'What? You would be stripped of your rank and court-martialled.'

I had nothing to lose: I wasn't in uniform.

'Answer my question,' he continued. 'You have a whole battalion. How are you going to deploy your troops?'

'I will dig in,' I said. 'I will let the enemy walk over. In the evening when they have settled down to their vodkas and bourbons, I will attack them in the rear with bayonets.'

The Captain shook his head and gave me up as a bad job. He said I would never make an officer, which was dis-heartening. He also told the class that the Headquarters' new recruitment policy was to be blamed for the deteriora-tion of the Army. Instead of recruiting officers from the warrior classes such as the Sikhs, Rajputs and Gurkhas, they had opened the doors to the scribes. He was particularly critical of the Intelligence Test, which counted for much with the Selection Board. 'Here you have a young man,' he said, pointing towards me, 'who has passed his Intelligence Test. And yet he cannot think of anything better than writing a letter to Army Headquarters, or digging in. If I had my way I would bury him six feet underground and put a tombstone on him to see that he doesn't get out.'

The class laughed, and each cadet looked at the instructor

as if he knew how to beat the shit out of the enemy.

By the end of the week, I got accustomed to the aches and the pains. Instinctively, I knew my left leg from my right; I could mark time as well as the Sergeant-Major himself, and I could double better than most cadets owing to the intensive training I had received from one and all. But I couldn't get used to living with the Gentlemen Cadets and I couldn't understand why they hated me so. I hoped that once my uniform was ready, I would not be so easily singled out as I was now; that should give me some respite. The tailor had measured me the day after I arrived, and I kept waiting anxiously for my battle-dress. Two weeks later when I got it, the damn thing was too tight for me, though I had lost twelve pounds. And the cloth was so rough that it irritated my skin. I detested the very sight of myself in it. But I didn't mind the uniform on others—in fact, they looked much smarter in khaki than in civvies. I asked the tailor to let out some cloth at the hips, but he refused. He predicted that within another week or two I might find the trousers a little on the loose side. And he wasn't far wrong.

I would have stayed in the Army and earned a place in history, for I was a good marksman. But my comrades-in-arms made my life impossible with their hate, malice and vulgarity. They all wanted to know if I had a sister to whom I would introduce them during the summer holidays. I told them I had nobody but an old mother, but they wouldn't believe me. The Hindus have a strange notion that Anglo-Indian girls are an easy catch. The Gentlemen Cadets wanted to know if I had slept with a woman. When I said I hadn't, they took me for a homosexual. One cadet asked me to shave him between his thighs. I refused. He said it was an order and I must obey.

I was kept so busy with parades, classes and fatigues that I hardly found time for anything else. When I did find time I would write down brief descriptions of people who had bully-ragged me, so that in the event of a war I could kill them. As I did not know the names of most of the people who tormented me, I had to make accurate notations on the colour of their hair, the shapes of their noses and chins, their gait, mannerisms, etc. The man I hated most was my Company Officer and I wrote a whole page on him. As misfortune would have it, he came across it while examining my cupboard. He had no difficulty in recognising himself from the lucid description I had given. And I had made the silly mistake of noting down the manner in which I intended to kill him.

The only part of the training I enjoyed was the sand-model class. And I must say this of the instructor, that he had an open mind and began to think better of me once I started putting less thought and more courage into solving the problems he posed me. He asked me what I would do if I were alone and unarmed and found myself surrounded by a platoon of Pakistani soldiers. I said I would address them at the top of my voice: 'You, you sons of Islam, you can kill me but you cannot kill the spirit of India. Mahatma Gandhi *ki jai* (victory to Mahatma Gandhi), *Bharat-mata ki jai* (victory to motherland).' On another occasion he asked me my plan of action were I to see a U.S. reconnaissance plane flying low and photographing our Prime Minister's bungalow. This was a tough question to answer and I spoilt it by thinking about it. I said I would get in touch with the American ambassador. The instructor reminded me that as an Army officer I had no business to talk politics. Later, it struck me that the correct strategy would be to shoo away the plane with my service revolver.

I resigned on a Monday, exactly four weeks after I had joined the Academy. I had given no thought to resigning, and it was a spontaneous gesture. If I hadn't been so sleepy that morning, I might have stayed on; if my comrades-in-arms had been a little kinder I might have got up for parade.

It happened this way.

As usual, the Company Officer kicked at my door at five and called me the penis of a donkey. I did not return the greeting with the customary 'Good morning sir'. I kept mum. He kicked at the door again, and called me other filthy names. But I maintained silence. After he had exhausted his Hindi vocabulary, I told him I had resigned from the Army.

'What? Who the hell are you trying to fool?'

'No one. I am telling you the truth.'

'Fuck off.'

'This evening. I am going to fuck off this evening, so you better leave me alone.'

'When did you resign?' he asked, a little less aggressively.

'This morning. I am writing my letter of resignation now.'

He gave the door a rattling kick, and thundered: 'Bloody bastard! Open the door, *ma ki choot* (cunt of your mother). Resigning! My bloody arse.'

As he went on abusing and kicking, I hurriedly wrote out my resignation on a large brown envelope. I remember every word of it: 'Dear Sir, After mature consideration I have come to the conclusion that the Army has nothing to offer me and I have nothing to offer the Army. Please accept my resignation with immediate effect and let me go home. Yours truly, Tristan Elliott.'

I slipped the letter out from beneath the door. The Company Officer read it and, after hurling a few more abuses, left. I guess he was getting late for parade.

I went back to bed. Three hours later a sepoy came and said that the Battalion Commander, Colonel Hans Raj, would like to see me in his office immediately. Without shaving or washing my face, I got into civvies and went. He spoke to me politely, but firmly.

'Why are you not in your uniform?'

'I have resigned, sir.'

'When did you resign?'

'This morning, sir.'

He looked at my letter of resignation. It was the only paper on his desk.

'Your resignation becomes effective only after Army Headquarters have accepted it. They may not accept it— they may take a month or more to accept it. Now you go back, get into your uniform, and report to your Company.'

'I can't, sir,' I said.

'What do you mean you can't? This is Army, my boy, not a . . .'

He didn't know how to finish the sentence. He muttered something under his breath, and again repeated his orders.

'I have had enough, sir,' I said. 'I am not going back, whatever might happen.'

'You will be court-martialled,' he shouted, losing his temper.

'It doesn't matter, sir. You can kill me but I am not going back. I have had enough of the Army.'

He stared at me hard, and I could see he was tense from the way his hand shook. I don't think he had ever met a man of my guts.

'All right. Go and wait in your room till you receive further orders from me.'

I returned to my room. I was furious at the thought that I had landed myself into a profession I couldn't get out of. What was the Army but downright slavery? And its rules violated the human rights in the Indian Constitution. I cursed Colonel Ross for painting a rosy picture of salutes, care of arms, mess, uniforms and all such nonsense.

At 1 p.m. the Battalion Commander sent for me again. I had shaved meanwhile, but was still in civvies.

'I have been in touch with Headquarters and they have agreed to release you. One of our trucks will be going to the station at six and you can get a lift.'

'Thank you, sir,' I said with emotion.

He did not reply.

Back in my room, I began to doubt the wisdom of my action. What would I do back home? How would I face my mother and Colonel Ross? What sort of a future awaited me? Who would give a job to a fellow who had fled from the Army? God, what had I done? And I felt I could never return to Delhi.

For two hours I fretted. I was in agony. The world seemed to have gone empty, suddenly. I had not experienced such a feeling of vacuity before. No, I could not leave the Army. I must stick it out, come what may. I went back to the Battalion Commander.

He looked at me pitifully, and shook his head. 'I have not come across a character like you,' he said. 'Make up your mind. I shall give you two hours. If you want to stay on, come and see me before 5 p.m. and I will phone up Headquarters and tell them you have withdrawn your letter of resignation. Now go back to your room and think.'

I thought, and thought. The more I thought the more confused I got. True, the option was before me. But what was I to choose? It was a terrible decision to make. If I stayed in the Army, I was stuck for good. And the very idea of spending my life with the Gentlemen Cadets chilled me. If I left the Army, what was I to do? What hopes of getting another job? And would another job be any the better? How would I face the people I knew in Delhi? I wish the Battalion Commander had not given me time to think. Thinking was torture. And each minute that passed brought me nearer a decision I could not take. I had never been in such anguish before.

Five minutes to five, I made up my mind. I was going to stay in the Army. I was going to bear every mortification my decision involved. I would suffer and suffer and suffer, but I would stay in the Army. I had at last made the choice—not even God could deter me now. I got into my uniform and rushed to the office of the Battalion Commander to tell him so. I knocked at his door.

'Wait a minute,' he called out. He was talking to someone.

'A minute!' I said to myself. 'You have just one minute to save yourself, Tristan. Within one minute you will see the Commander and withdraw your resignation. And then for the rest of your days you will be what your Company Officer calls you: the penis of a donkey. Get out, while there is time. Run, Tristan, run; run for your life.'

I ran. I threw all my clothes into my suitcase and sent for a taxi. After I had boarded the train and it had begun moving, the magnitude of my action and of the day's doings crystallised before me. I had blundered. I had lost forever the one chance to make a success of my life. I would now finish up on the rubbish heap.

I opened the door of the compartment. I leaned forward, holding the handles on either side of the door. I could throw myself out. I would be dead, and there would be neither the past nor the future to think about. It could easily be done, and I felt I had the courage to do it. I could do it right now.

All I had to do was to open the palms of my hands.

I closed the door and came back to my seat. I was no longer grieving over what I had done. I was no longer afraid of what might happen to me. A man who has the strength to die has the strength to live.

'And so, Marie, I am here with you today. What do you think of my story?'

'As a story it is quite good. But you will have to improve your English,' Marie said.

'What's wrong with my English?'

'It's too simple—babyish. Even a Grade Nine student could understand it. And you keep using the same words. At one place you used the word "thought" three times! Why not use other words like "cogitate"?'

Marie is a hard critic. And that's what I need if I'm going to set myself high standards.

26

Marie thinks I need more practice in writing, that though my ideas are good there is a lot of room for improvement in style. She has suggested that I should take after Shakespeare (especially *Julius Caesar*), but I asked her if that wouldn't be a little too ambitious. 'Not at all,' she said. 'Unless you aim high, you get nowhere.' I told her I couldn't model myself on Shakespeare and would she suggest another writer. She said she would think about it. Meanwhile, I shouldn't waste my time but write as best as I could: about my earliest recollections of childhood. I told her there was nothing in my childhood to write about. To this she replied that 'The child is Father of the man', and all great writers must start at the beginning. So I wrote the following account for my love, who loves me.

I have hazy recollections of Father. He was like me, tall and slim and exceedingly handsome. I recall having seen him only two or three times, so there are few memories that stick to the mind. He used to throw me in the air and catch me as if I were a cricket ball. He would walk with his legs apart, and make me walk between them. I think it made him feel big. He would play with me and my toys, and then, suddenly losing all interest, he would get into his car and drive away. That's all I remember about him.

When he was away, I used to ask Mother when Daddy would be back. She always gave the same answer, 'Very soon, my child.' We had fallen into a set pattern: the same questions and the same answers. But I liked asking the question, not because I missed Daddy, but because Mother always kissed me after I'd asked.

I remember the fateful evening well. Mother and I were having ice-cream after dinner, when the phone rang. Mother got up lazily and picked it up. She listened intently for a moment and then gave a piercing wail and dropped it. She ran and took me up in her arms.

'Your Daddy won't come back,' she wept bitterly, pressing me to her bosom.

'Why?' I asked.

'God! O my God!' she moaned.

I did not know what had happened. I did not feel sorry for Mother, for I had never seen her in such a state before.

Soon our house was overflowing with visitors, mostly men in uniforms. Mother had regained some of her composure, though she still sobbed spasmodically. The visitors were all very kind to me; they all wanted to play with me and asked me what toys I'd like to have. No one before had been as kind as the whole neighbourhood was that evening. I was happy, in spite of Mother's grief. It didn't matter if Daddy wasn't coming back. I didn't know he was dead. If they had all sung out that he was dead, I wouldn't have understood.

For a week the elders made much of me. I was the most wanted boy in the neighbourhood. People wouldn't let me walk: they would lift me up in their arms as soon as they saw me. And everybody kissed me. I liked being kissed. I stopped asking Mummy when Daddy would return.

People got tired of me, and soon I was back with Mummy asking the old question.

'Your Daddy won't come,' she would say in tears.

I didn't like to see Mummy cry. But mentioning Daddy always brought me a kiss.

Then an aunt of mine told me that I mustn't speak about Daddy to Mummy, that my Daddy had gone to heaven.

'How did he go to heaven?' I asked.

'In an aeroplane,' said my aunt.

'Like my aeroplane?' I asked, running and fetching my blue-and-white one which Daddy had given me.

'No, it was much bigger.'

I told Mummy I would like to go to Heaven in an aeroplane. She hugged me and wept, and made me promise never to say it again.

'But I want to be with my Daddy,' I persisted.

'So do I, my child,' she sobbed.

'Let's go then, Mummy,' I said, tugging at her petticoat.

'Your Daddy is dead.'

'What is that, Mummy?'

'You will understand when you grow up, Tristan.'

A year later, when I started going to school, I began to understand. I wasn't sorry about it, but I was afraid Mother might leave me and go away like Daddy. And then what would I do? I couldn't live alone, I had no money and no one was willing to give me a job. And the servants didn't listen to me. I begged Mummy not to leave me alone and go away. I promised her I would be good if she took me with her.

Mother and I used to sleep together: sometimes in the same bed, but always in the same room. Then a man began visiting Mother, and I would be alone in the bedroom till late at night. I was afraid Mother might go away with the man, and so I wouldn't close my eyes even for a minute until she came to bed. When I felt very frightened, I would tip-toe to the door and watch Mother through the key-hole. One night I saw her holding the man close to herself the way she held me. I didn't like it; I walked straight into the living-room.

'Who is he?' I asked.

Mother pulled her hands away immediately and stood up. The man looked at me first, and then at her.

'Go to your bed,' Mother said sharply.

'Who is he?' I asked again.

'Go back to your bed,' she shouted, and took me by the arm and locked me in the bedroom.

I wept. It wasn't Mother holding the man which frightened me, but the way she spoke to me. She no longer loved me, I thought. She will now leave me surely. And what will I do?

Two hours later, when Mother came to sleep, I was still awake and sobbing. She kissed me and asked me not to cry. I said I wouldn't cry if she told me who the man was.

136

'He is a good friend,' said Mother.

'I don't like him,' I said, sulkily.

'He is a nice man, and he is going to bring you toys. Now you go to sleep.'

'He is not a nice man and I don't want his toys. I won't sleep if he comes here.'

I never saw him again. I don't know if Mother ever saw him again. I would have forgotten him if it were not that he came to live in my mind as the first of my mother's male friends.

I liked school. The girls looked nice in their green-and-white uniforms. I liked sitting near them and touching them whenever I could. I liked playing with them during the lunch break, but some of them didn't want to play with me. They would ask me to go and play with the boys. There was one girl I wished I had as a sister. She was tall and thin with dark hair done up in two pig-tails. She and I would go searching for butterflies, and when we were alone she would kiss me. It was a nice feeling, different from when Mother kissed me.

My childhood was happy, except for the fear that Mother might leave me. This fear lasted until I was fourteen. It was not that many men came to our house, but those who did come appeared sinister to me. I saw through them: not one of them really cared for me, all they sought was to take Mother away from me. They brought me toys and sweets, but didn't want me around when Mother was there. They would ruffle my hair indifferently, pat me on the cheek, give me a rupee, and ask me to go out and play. If Mother didn't happen to be in the house, or was getting dressed to go out, then they would talk to me. And they asked the same questions: Do you have many visitors? When does your mother get up in the mornings? Are you going anywhere for the holidays?

Looking back, I don't think any of my mother's friends were really serious about her. And I am sure Mother never was, except about Belton. Belton was a widower who held a good job with the railways. He had a nondescript face, made memorable by a large scar on his right cheek. The scar was like a barometer: it was the most accurate reflection of his moods. When it turned scarlet, I kept outdoors.

Belton hated me, and he made no pretences about it. He rarely talked to me, or inquired what I was doing. His daughter Sheila, who was two years older than I, also hated me. She used to beat me with the belt of her uniform. She would chase me all over the playground, whipping me as one whips a horse. At times I used to cry. I was only nine years old.

'Why do you beat me?' I asked her one day, swallowing my boyish pride.

'Because your mummy is taking my daddy away,' she said.

'How?'

'Tell your mummy to leave my daddy alone.'

That evening I told Mummy what Sheila had said. Her face lost colour. I asked her if she was really going away with Belton. She did not reply, but left me saying she was going to work and would be late coming home.

In the nearby jail the gongs struck every half hour. I lay in bed counting the hours and praying to God to send back my mummy soon. I was trembling when the hour struck twelve. Mother had left me, and from tomorrow I would have to fend for myself.

I heard the door open, and then I heard Mother's footsteps. I felt relieved. I heard Belton's voice and it worried me. For once he was speaking softly so as not to disturb me.

They were in the living-room, speaking in hushed voices. Why were they being so cautious? Were they discussing me? Had Mother come to collect her things? She would have to come to the bedroom to pack her clothes. I must keep awake.

'Send him away. Send him anywhere,' Belton bawled out.

'He has done nothing,' protested my mother.

My fears had come true. I could no longer stay in bed. Bare-footed I ran to Mother and sat down beside her, with my arms round her.

'Please don't send me away,' I begged.

'Get out,' shouted Belton.

'Leave him alone,' said Mother.

'Get out of here,' shouted Belton again. And he caught me by the collar and dragged me into the middle of the room. With a push he sent me staggering forward so that I fell on my face. I howled.

'Don't touch my boy,' asserted Mother, as Belton moved menacingly towards me.

'You are encouraging that brat. He is completely spoilt ... if I had my way I'd beat the piss out of him,' roared Belton.

'He has done nothing,' contended Mother

'Nothing? To disobey orders is nothing? Is this how you bring up a child?' retorted Belton.

'He is fatherless,' moaned Mother.

'It's time he bloody well had a father,' sneered Belton.

Mother's defence gave me courage. I rolled over and lay on my back, returning Belton's cruel stare. Between tears, I raved: 'Go away. You are not wanted here . . . go away and leave me with my mummy. Go to Sheila . . . go away with Sheila. Sheila beats me because of you.'

No sooner had I mentioned Sheila than the red scar on his face became redder. But for once it did not frighten me. He came and hovered above me with closed fists, ordering me to get up. I knew that if I stood up he would knock me down again. He nudged me in the ribs with his toes, shouting, 'Get up, get up you swine. I shall count ten, and if you don't stand up before then I'll break your head. One—two—three . . .'

Before he had counted six, I had caught hold of his leg with both my hands and bit deep into his calf. He yelled with pain as I drew blood out of him. The sight of Belton's blood made me proud and angry. Now that I had tasted his blood, It wouldn't matter even if he killed me.

Mother intervened and managed to separate us. She ordered me to go back to bed. As I was leaving, Belton landed a hard kick on my back which sent me flying out of the room.

I could hear Mother and Belton arguing fiercely, but could not follow what they were accusing each other of. Then suddenly I heard Mother shriek hysterically, and a shiver went up my spine. As I trembled, I heard the sound of a slap and the slamming of doors. Mother came rushing in and fell on top of me.

'What is it, Mummy?'

'It is all right, my darling, it is all right now,' she sobbed.

I viewed Mother with detachment. I seemed to have lost all sympathy for her. 'Do you love Belton, Mummy?'

'Yes, Tristan. I love him very much. But I will not give you up for the whole world . . . not for the whole world.'

'Do you love him more than you loved Daddy?'

'Don't, Tristan, don't ask that.'

'If Daddy were alive today, I wouldn't have been kicked.'

'Oh, my boy, forgive me. Forgive your poor old mother. No one shall ever touch you again,' she wept. And I had not seen her weep so bitterly since Father's death.

For five years after this incident, I do not recall seeing any man in our house staying past eleven. When Mother started dating again, there were furrows on her beautiful face and loose flesh on her arms and thighs. I felt sorry for her, for I had learnt to sense her loneliness. As I grew older, I realised how idle my fears had been: Mother could never have left me. And then I saw the need to leave her and let her live her own life.

I shouldn't read this to Marie. Apart from my English, what would she think of my mother? How would I explain to her another's loneliness? And that love for me, for which my mother must always be alone.

27

There seems to be no end to my sorrows. If there ever was a Man of Sorrows, it's me. Marie leaves for Vancouver tomorrow, and I am broken-hearted. As I sat with a broken heart in the back-yard, watching Marie paint the fence red (she feels we should leave the house in good shape for the Mises), an R.C.M.P. officer stopped by. He said it was a routine check, but I didn't believe him. And when he asked me what I did for a living, I stretched out my hands towards him so that he might handcuff me. But Marie's presence of mind saved me: she told him I was a professor and a writer. After that the officer kept addressing me as 'sir' and I soon regained my former stature. I am very frightened of policemen: it's a hangover from my days in India. And the police in Canada have not been unduly kind to me. On one occasion they stopped me from breaking the window of my own car to get to the keys I had locked in by mistake. On another occasion they tried to book me for drunken driving because I smelled of alcohol. I had some difficulty explaining that I hadn't consumed a drop of liquor—that the smell originated elsewhere. I had dabbed some whisky under my armpits as I had run out of cologne water.

When the policeman had left, Marie said she would wash and iron my clothes. So we went to the basement. While scrubbing the coffee stains off my pyjamas, she said she would like to have a baby by me. This gave me a scare. Now I am not against babies at all, but a few days ago Marie had said that there had been insanity in her family. One of her granduncles wrote letters to Queen Victoria proposing marriage, and an aunt of hers still pees standing upright. She is the Vice-President of the local branch of the Women's Libera-

141

tion Movement.

I sought comfort in the thought that one should leave something to God. After all, He was being kind to me and He hadn't given me Marie only to bestow a dud on me. That would cost Him my gratitude. And why should the baby take after her mother or her mother's family? Why not after me—the father? Even if it had a drop or two of my blood, surely that would counteract all unhealthy influences. Besides, the Canadians are so neutral: they are neither sane nor insane, good nor bad. They generally take the colour from their surroundings.

Don't think I am being unkind. I love Canada and the Canadians—more so since I met Marie. Where else could I have been a professor? Where else could I have found a girl like Marie? Where else could I have had free medical treatment? True, they knocked my eye out, but I didn't have to pay for it except the modest deterrent fee. And as soon as I got out of the hospital, the doctor gave me a certificate which qualified me for the salary continuance insurance plan. I would have qualified for the death benefits, too, had my lovely Marie not turned up. Canada is the country for me, and an Anglo-Indian-Canadian child is what this country needs. It needs fresh, oriental blood, not something that has grown up in hot-houses and been kept in cold storage. Farm chickens are hard to come by, but they are worth the trouble.

Twenty minutes after Marie had expressed her desire to have my baby, I agreed. By then Marie had forgotten all about the baby. She was now more interested in my getting a divorce and marrying her.

'When do you think you can get a divorce?' she asked.

'Damn the divorce,' I said. 'I am not going down on bended knees to Elsa.'

'How will you marry me, then?'

'Like everybody else.'

'We can't get married till you are divorced.'

'Marie, let's not meddle with it then. Marriages are made in heaven, anyway,' I said.

'I don't know what you are talking about,' exploded Marie.

'I know it is difficult for you to understand, not knowing Elsa. I have a hunch it is not worth approaching Elsa for a divorce. We must take the initiative into our own hands.'

Marie felt I was trying to evade the question of marriage. I swore I was hers for all time, and that I would not have her entertaining such foolish doubts. I assured her I was prepared to marry her this very minute, and for her sake had even given up the idea of dying.

Marie asked me where we should go for our honeymoon. I reminded her that we ought to deal with one thing at a time. My own preference was to begin with marriage as that was the most important thing.

'Let's plan our marriage straight away,' I said. 'I don't want you to doubt my intentions. Would you like to invite your folks to our wedding?'

'Of course,' she replied. 'What about you? Whom would you like?'

I hadn't given the matter a thought. But then I had few friends in Canada.

'I'd like the Peabodys. Look, I could ask Horace to give us one of his "wedding poems". We could get it printed in gold letters on the invitation cards.'

'That would be nice. Would he write one for us?'

'Horace would lay down his life for me, Marie. But he won't have to write a poem for us: he has written scores of them and he would allow me my pick. It is his "divorce poems" which are copyrighted.'

'What sort of poetry does he write?'

'Very intellectual. When sending them to magazines, he always includes a prose paraphrase of each poem. One editor rejected his poem but published the paraphrase.'

'Do you think we should also publish the paraphrase?'

'What a brilliant idea, Marie. We could print the paraphrase on the back of the card, and put a little note under the poem: "For clue, see reverse side." Better still, don't print the paraphrase, but offer a prize to the person who can get the correct meaning of the poem. It will keep the guests busy during the ceremony.'

After finalising our wedding arrangements, we came and sat on the sofa. Marie tried to mend my broken heart with words of wisdom and courage. She promised to send for me within a month, as soon as she had found a room big enough to hold the two of us. She wants a place near Cruickshanks on Georgia Street—the firm for which she will be book-keeping. She has asked me to lead a normal life, that is to walk to the River Quimperle every day. I said it would be getting cold, and I didn't have a car. She is looking forward to my becoming famous. She has presented me with an illustrated dictionary, and is going to send me a copy of Shakespeare.

Marie lectured me a lot. I wish she hadn't on our last day, when I was feeling low. She accused me of being hyper-critical—especially towards people from whom I have re-ceived nothing except kindness. I didn't ask her to specify, I tend to agree with her. I do feel at times I can't be a wholly integrated personality, or I wouldn't be reacting so violently to my environment—especially the seasons. If I were pure, the purity of the winter snow would thrill me. The birds twitter, the hare limps over the frozen grass, while I sit on my arse condemning man and nature alike. I told Marie what I thought of myself. She admonished me for being so self-critical.

As night approached, Marie stood up to leave. 'Tristan, it is time for me to say goodbye. Look after yourself, if only for my sake.'

'I will, Marie.'

'My Tristan, you will never know what great happiness it has been loving you. It is so wonderful to love a person like you.'

'Don't say such things. It hurts me,' I said. 'We must part like men of steel.'

'Yes, my love.'

'Marie, I want you to give me something to remember you by.'

'Anything.'

'I want your left stocking.'

'But I'll be cold walking home.'

'Don't worry. I shall walk you home.'

'How will that help?'

'Please, I must have your left stocking.'

Marie took off her stocking and gave it to me. There were holes in it, and the disappointment showed on my face.

'Why, Tristan? Don't you want it now?'

'Give me the right one,' I said. 'There are holes in this one.'

'You are not going to wear it, Tristan!'

'Please don't contradict me on the last day. Can you not fulfil my one small wish?'

Marie took off her right stocking and gave it to me. There were no holes in it. I asked her to put on the left one. She said it would look silly walking down the road with one stocking on, but I convinced her it would be some protection against the cold.

'One last request, Marie,' I begged.

'All right,' she sighed.

'Give me your handkerchief.'

'I don't have one.'

'Then give me your Kleenex.'

'I don't have any.'

'Well, I'll get one from the kitchen and you can blow your nose in it and leave it on the table.'

'You are completely mad, Tristan.'

I was very hurt. To be madly in love, and then to be called mad by the very person you love. Can there be anything more painful?

'Come now. I didn't mean it,' coaxed Marie. 'It's getting late.'

I walked her home with my arm round her waist. She shivered all the same. When we reached her place she gave me a quick kiss, and ran in.

28

Letters—letters—letters. Morning and evening letters. Letters every day, sometimes as many as two. I am her 'Most loving Tristan', 'Darling of darlings' and 'Dearest of all'. And she signs off: 'Yours with love, love, and more love, Marie.'

The letters are full of vows, and promissory notes of love of historic (and literary) significance. I sit for whole days reading and re-reading them. I know them: comma, colon and all. There is no full-stop to love such as ours. Here is what my Marie writes:

> It's past noon now; the day is moving slowly, I am trying to gather my spirits by being occupied with things around me. I can't imagine that we won't be together this evening, and tomorrow and the day after. But I hope that day is not far off when I shall be with you again, forever and ever, till the last of my days.
>
> I have so many wonderful memories of you, that will help me to live thro' the days I am alone. Believe me or not, I cannot think of a single person in my life who has been so dear to me as you have been.
>
> I keep missing you all the time; how can I really be happy? I really must be closer to you, at least within your reach. I just want to make you happy and be with you when you need me.
>
> I wish I could stretch my hands out that far, that I could hold your hand. But I shall wait till you are here to do that.
>
> You just have to be here with me. I do know one

thing: I can never ever break off my tie and bond to you. You don't know what it has been for me—meeting people, being with them on the surface and mentally being with you all the time: body, soul and mind. I just have this firm feeling and belief about you in me, and, no matter what happens in the future, I shall go on living with this feeling. It is the only thing that keeps me going.

I was so glad to get your letter. Just before I got your letter my mind was in a whirl of images about you. I have come to realise that you are not simply a person I love, but an entire world to me. And it is in this world I plan to submerge myself. Every day, countless hours pass by, with me thinking of you, you are so much a part of me . . .

Joe called me to dinner last night. I think I spoiled his evening when I told him how much you meant to me. It was his fault, for he asked if I loved anybody, and then I went on to say how much I loved you. Poor Joe kept mumbling and stumbling with words, and very sarcastically said, 'How come you are not in Corwind with Tristan!' I said I had my own plans which I didn't have to disclose to him!

It is so good to hear from you. You are so much 'in' and 'around' me. I need not even eat—I've used up all my appetite just for you.

I feel deliriously happy. I have a feeling you will be with me very soon. I promise with all my heart I shall be good to you. . . . I want to yell out, so you can hear me! I feel so 'high', so drunk with happiness at the mere thought of you.

It was inevitable that Marie should fall for me the way she did. Except for the whore in London, no woman has been able to resist me. That's the way with women: they lack self-control. But they are not altogether to blame when they meet a man like me. I am firmly in the saddle now. Before I go to Vancouver I shall write a nice letter to Elsa telling her how much Marie loves me, and wishing her the very best in life.

29

There she lies. Lily white. On the bedroom floor. She ascended to heaven with the first shot, nevertheless I fired two more to make sure she didn't trip on the way. Wasn't necessary though, for she sagged into a heap at the first shot. But taking aim, I had shut my good eye by mistake. Perfectionist that I am, I took no risks: there are three clean bullet marks just below the window. There will be cartridges to spare after I have tidied her and stretched her on the bed with myself beside her. And a hole through my heart.

I went to see her as soon as I got Marie's letter. She was in the store helping her mother. I beckoned her to one side with my hand.

'There is bad news from your sister, Marion.'

'What is it?' she gasped.

'I can't tell you here. No one must know. Come to my place immediately—as fast as you can.'

'Not now! I can't . . .'

'Not a word to your mother,' I interrupted her.

I left her gaping. I ran back and made my bed. Fresh white linen. I lit an incense stick that Marie had brought for me. I loaded the magazine of my rifle and placed it in the drawer.

Marion came panting, breathless. She was quivering.

'What has happened to sis?'

'Easy, Marion, she is still alive,' I said to soothe her nerves as I led her to the bedroom.

'Tell me—tell me now. Don't keep me guessing.'

'Don't guess. Here, read this.' And I gave her Marie's letter.

I could see Marion's eyes dart swiftly over the lines. Then

she looked at me, puzzled.

'Read it aloud, Marie,' I said, quietly.

'Why do you look at me like that? And I am not Marie!'

'Read it, Marion. Aloud,' I said.

She read: 'Dear Tristan, I think I must be frank and honest with you and tell you that I feel we cannot come together as we had planned. You are very dear to me, but I finally realised after much contemplation, fear, embarrassment and anxiety, that we are not suited for one another. I have been seeing Joe lately, and I shall be moving into his apartment next week till I find something suitable for myself. I shall pray to God to give you courage to face life: you have so much to live for and so much to give to the world. Love, Marie.'

'I am sorry for you,' said Marion.

'I don't doubt that. We pass the word along as if we were playing ball. I was sorry for my mother and Nellie, and then Heather and my wife and . . .'

'Your wife? You are married?'

'Your sister. She was sorry for me. And Elsa too, when I lost my eye. All of us sorry for one another, as if the world could be saved by mere apologies. All my life . . . it is difficult to explain. But, you know, something could be done, if we would but do it. It needs courage and strength. The road is dark and long, but we must walk it, for there is no other road. . . . We must light it for the sake of those who must walk after us. Our act might seem insignificant, but it will be the first step taken in the march of a thousand miles. Mahatma Gandhi purified himself by taking a bath on the seashores of Dandi. Then he picked up a lump of natural salt, and thereby defied the British Government. People laughed—but the act was symbolic.'

'I don't understand! What has Gandhi to do with me?'

'You too have to purify yourself. Go into the bathroom and use the sandalwood soap. I shall bring the towel. Hurry, the incense is burning out.'

'What? Are you all right?'

'Get into the bath, Marion. That's my last stick of incense.'

'You are mad! O God, why did I come here? Let me go.'

She tried to force her way out, but I stood blocking the door. When she pushed me, I pushed her back. She went staggering against the wall.

'What do you want from me?' she asked, frightened.

'The two of us can yet save the world.'

'I am not surprised my sister left you. You are mad!'

'Your sister did not think me mad. She entrusted the world to my care. There—in that letter: "You have much to give to the world." '

'And what, may I ask, do you have to give to the world?' she mocked.

Here was the eternal confrontation between the cynic and the saviour. Would she understand? Would the paschal lamb understand why it must be slaughtered and its blood smeared on the lintels of Israel? And yet the saviour must speak the truth.

'Salvation,' I said.

'What?'

'Salvation,' I repeated.

Marion laughed, but the laugh was a frightened one. She made another frantic bid to get past me, and once again I pushed her back. She stood transfixed, awfully pale.

'The incense has burnt out, and you have not yet purified yourself.'

'I'll run home and get you some incense.'

'I may be mad, but I am no fool, Marie.'

'I am not Marie—I'm Marion. Let me go!' she shouted. But she did not move towards the door.

'Marie, or Marion, or Heather or Elsa. They are all one in God's eye. Except that the lamb should be of undoubted virginity. I hope you are a virgin.'

'You pig. You dirty old man,' raved Marion.

'And some began to spit on Him, and to cover His face. And they blindfolded Him, and asked Him, saying, Prophesy: who is he that struck thee? And many other things spake they against Him, reviling Him.'

'O God, where am I?' Marion wept.

Peace, Marion, peace. Jesus turning unto them said, Daughters of Jerusalem, weep not for me, but weep for yourselves, and for your children. For behold, the days are coming, in which they shall say, Blessed are the barren, and the wombs that never bare, and the breasts that never gave suck.'

'What do you want?'

'I want from you a supreme sacrifice—a sacrifice as great as Alcestis made for Admetus.'

'I don't understand . . . I don't.'

'Alcestis gave her life to preserve that of her husband. But Admetus lived to pass pollution on. The sin is in the womb —the womb has to be destroyed.'

'How?'

'By your death.'

'You don't mean that?'

'Without the shedding of blood there is no remission.'

'You won't kill me! O God, you won't kill me!'

'Don't be afraid. I shall kill myself too—after you.'

I took out the gun from the drawer. Marion froze with terror. No wonder she looked so white in death.

'Don't, don't, Tristan. Do anything but don't kill me. O God, deliver us.'

'Deliver us. Deliver us. In all the streets in all the cities they are crying: Deliver us. The hapless, the homeless, the blind and the maimed: they are all crying the same thing. Now is the time to deliver mankind. Let God create another world, let Him water another garden, fashion another Adam, take another rib, devise another snake. Till then, let there be peace. Till then, let not our sins visit our children. It is only a beginning. We can do no more.'

'Don't kill me. Do anything you want with me but don't kill me.' And she spoke to me tenderly, 'You want to make love to me, Tristan, don't you? I love you. Come, come now; lie down here beside me.'

'Are you ready, Marion?' I asked quietly, lifting the gun to my shoulder. I couldn't bear to see her plead.

'They will hang you for a murderer,' she cried in a final bid to deter me.

'On the third day I shall rise to heaven as easily from the gallows as I shall from the grave,' I said.

These were my last words. I felt I could not have spoken more truly.

Marion tried to flee by climbing out of the window. She had grabbed on to the sill and was heaving herself up when I fired.

I must go now. I must keep my promise to Marion. The angels of God are waiting for me. The red carpet is laid out for me, and all heaven has assembled to receive me. Daddy will pilot my blue-and-white plane. As I step out my Company Officer will give the signal for a thirty-gun salute. After I have inspected the guard of honour, I shall walk up to my Company Officer and remind him how he used to call me *ghada-ka-lund*. I shall intercede on his behalf and on the behalf of all damned souls. There is no hate in me now— I am all love. I shall choose a bride in heaven, and send for Peabody to recite one of his marriage odes. I shall paraphrase it for the Almighty.

I am coming, my Lord. I am going, Elsa. Goodbye, Elsa.

Heaven forbid! Where is Marion! I surely could not have missed with all three shots! The window is open! Horror of horrors! The body-snatchers have been here. They have taken my body from me. They have not left even one drop of the sacrificial blood where she lay. I must send for the police —before the medicos chop her into bits. The police! Elsa, phone the police—999. Elsa, goodbye—Goodbye, Elsa.

Q4